BEVERLY HILLS, 90210

BEVERLY HILLS, 90210

BEGINNINGS

BY
LAWRENCE CROWN

B⊕XTREE

BASED ON THE TELEVISION
SERIES CREATED BY DARREN STAR

The stories in this book are
based on teleplays by Darren
Star, Charles Rosin, David
Stenn and Amy Spies.

First published in the UK 1991
by BOXTREE LIMITED, 36 Tavistock Street,
London WC2E 7PB

5 7 9 10 8 6 4

© 1991 Torand, a Spelling Ent. Co.
All rights reserved

Cover photograph: Andrew Semel
Photo courtesy: Fox Broadcasting Company

Cover design: Titan Studio

1–85283–680–6

Typeset by Cambrian Typesetters, Frimley, Surrey
Printed and bound in Great Britain by Cox & Wyman Ltd., Reading, Berkshire

Except in the United States of America, this book is sold subject to the condition that it shall not, by way of trade or otherwise, be lent, resold, hired out or otherwise circulated without the publisher's prior consent in any form of binding or cover other than that in which it is published and without a similar condition including this condition being imposed on a subsequent purchaser.

A catalogue record for this book is available from the British Library

Special thanks to *Noreen* for sharing her recollections and to *Darren Star* for writing such an excellent source script.

PROLOGUE

MINNESOTA FAREWELL

The lake shore constantly changes, Brenda Walsh thought, because of all the work the beavers do.

She eyed the teethmarks on the birch stump about twenty feet from the water's edge and the muddy trail of matted grass meandering down to the marshy part of the lake. In the summer months the beavers were *always* busy.

Nature's architects, her father called them. She swatted at a fat August mosquito, remembering childhood weekends here on Big Boy Lake, sitting for hours with her father and brother and watching the beavers build their great dam.

Barefoot and bare-legged, her auburn hair whipped by a warm late afternoon wind, she wandered along the sandy shore to the rickety little dock in front of their weekend summer home, a real log cabin that her father's father had built with his own hands.

Her brother and her father were out in the canoe, paddling in. 'Hey, Bren,' Brandon shouted. 'Lookit! Dinner!'

She squinted against the dancing lights on the blue water. He was holding up a walleye. It was quite an accomplishment because at this time of year the fishing wasn't good.

In this late summer heat there was too much *natural* food, and the fish were too busy jumping at the mosquitoes buzzing around above the lake to take notice of even the finest, most cunning bait. But in another month, Brenda knew, the leaves would turn and begin to drop off the trees, the mosquitoes would disappear and the fish would be striking again.

'Nice goin', Brandon,' she shouted back through cupped hands. 'Looks like ten pounds.'

'At least,' her brother's voice came back across the water, 'and the lake hasn't even turned yet.'

In another month, when cool weather and the first frosts came, she knew, the waters in the lake would 'turn' and the fish would dive to the warmth of their familiar deep holes, where the wiliest of the old fishermen knew they could find them. It was a trick Brenda and Brandon had known since they were old enough to throw out a drop line and sinker with a bobber. Gramps had taught them.

This lake reminded her of him, and of her childhood. There wasn't a place her eye could see that didn't bring back memories:

. . . The three small elm and birch-covered islands in the middle of the lake, where she and Brandon used to go to play pirates and Swiss Family Robinson.

. . . The stand of aspen on the eastern shore where the golden eagles had their nest. They mated for life, gramps had told her one day, when they were out fishing and two of the eagles, their great wings outspread, were riding an updraft overhead. Three summers before, she'd chased a hunter away, just as he was taking aim at the female of her favourite mated pair. *How dare you try to kill Harriet!* she'd wailed, *What would Ozzie and the kids do? ... They mate for life, they live as long as we do! ... Don't you understand?* The hunter, some tourist who really hadn't a clue, had beat a hasty retreat, pursued by her withering scorn.

... The reedy marshlands on the western side of the lake, their size almost doubled now because of the beaver dam, where she and Brandon once paddled to gather wild rice, shaking it into the canoe just like the Chippewa Indians used to do. Only, they'd overloaded theirs and nearly sank. To this day, she still teased her brother about how he'd jumped overboard 'to lighten the load' and had come up gasping and sputtering, only to realize that he was standing in water that was just waist-deep.

Here, the memories were alive, as alive as the silvery pike cutting through crystalline water, the majestic eagles soaring through the endless blue summer sky and the fat beavers waddling up on shore.

But in their new home, in faraway Beverly Hills, would the memories fade? Would her dreamy childhood idyll be replaced by new, harder-edged California dreams?

*

Dinner was delicious – pan-fired pike, hand-gathered wild rice, tomatoes from their own garden – but unusually subdued, as if even their parents, Cindy and Jim, had finally realized that this was it, their last night at the lake, and who knew when, or *if*, the family would be here together again.

Their mother, of course, tried to lighten the mood by talking about their new lives and what they expected from Beverly Hills. 'I'm looking forward to making new friends,' she said, determinedly upbeat, 'and to summer all year around. . . . How about you, Jim?'

'That's easy,' their father said. 'No more travelling. We'll be spending a lot more time together, I expect.'

Brandon affected nonchalance. For Mister Popularity, things would just continue on in the same winning groove as they were in now: Sports Editor at the school paper, varsity track, good grades . . . 'Oh yeah, *blondes*,' he added. 'I expect there'll be a lot more of those in my life from now on. Not your Minnesota-type pale blonde, y'know, but the *real California thing* . . . I'm talkin' no tan lines here.'

'*Gross*,' Brenda exclaimed, making a disgusted face, before saying something about new friends and new challenges, the sort of things she expected her parents wanted to hear, but it wasn't what she was really thinking at all.

The truth was, she was tired of living in Brandon's shadow, being treated like Mister Popularity's younger sister, even though they were twins and the same age. And she was tired of being shy and proper.

She knew her reputation: a cute *kid*, but kind of a drone. Secretly, she was determined to change all that. And even though she loved Minnesota and she loved the lake, this move was her big chance to create a new life, a new identity, and she truly intended to make the most of it.

*

'Wake up, Brandon! Hurry up!'

'Huh? . . . Go away, Bren.' Brandon squinted at the illuminated dial of his alarm on the nightstand next to his bunk. 'Jeez, it's three in the morning,' he groaned.

'Leave me alone. We gotta be up in three more hours for the drive back and then we gotta finish packing, and then we fly away . . .' His sleep-slurred voice drifted off.

Brenda shook him again. 'C'*mon*! You gotta see this!'

'Wha–' Brandon struggled awake. There was his sister, standing over him in her 'nightshirt,' actually an old plaid shirt she'd commandeered from their father, and her face was suffused with an excited glowing light.

He peered sleepily around: Waitaminute, he thought, the entire room was suffused with glowing light. But not the delicate pearly light of a full moon; no, this was almost *red*.

'What's goin' on?'

'The Lights,' she whispered. 'Come outside and see.'

Brandon shrugged into jeans and a tee shirt, ran a hand through his sleep-mussed hair and padded barefoot outdoors after his sister.

What Minnesota teenager doesn't know about the *aurora borealis*, the Northern Lights? Brandon and Brenda had had the dictionary definition drummed into them at school: *a luminous phenomenon visible in the northernmost reaches of the Northern Hemisphere, consisting of streamers or arches of light appearing in the upper atmosphere of the earth's arctic polar regions and caused by the emission of light from atoms excited by electrons accelerated along the planet's magnetic field lines.*

And what Minnesota teenager hadn't seen the Northern Lights at least once? But not like this. Never like this.

Usually, the Lights were a few ghostly wisps of whitish light in the night sky. But tonight . . .

The immense sky, in every direction, was a fairyland of dancing light – and not merely ghostly white, but *colours*, the like of which they'd never seen – streamers of Pepto Bismol pink, liquid rivers of hot magenta and gleaming gold.

And it was all in motion, constantly changing and shifting. And the streamers of light rose undulating to a common vanishing point, way above their awestruck, upturned faces, far out in the blackness of the night sky.

'God!' Brandon whispered. 'It's like this gigantic teepee made outta light!'

'And we're right under the middle of it!'

'Incredible!'

'Look, it's all reflected on the water, too.'

It was a spectacle unparalleled, and after watching it for an hour or more in utter silence, they went in and awakened their parents, who grumbled at first, but then came out, too, to be dazzled.

And all four of them sat out there, on the verge between the molten lake and the molten sky, entranced, until the pastel glow of dawn and the mocking yodels of a flight of passing loons washed the ineffable *aurora borealis* away.

CHAPTER ONE

The white, two-storey Spanish-style house on Hillcrest, an oak-shaded residential street above busy Sunset Boulevard, was wrapped in early morning quiet. Now that the For Sale sign was gone and the burly, sweaty movers had departed, it looked like any other house on the peacefully slumbering block. With its wide expanse of green lawn and neatly trimmed hedges, it could have been the all-American, middle class home on the all-American, middle class block. You half expected to see Beaver Cleaver bound out the front door.

Only the cars in the driveways here were all BMWs and Mercedes, and property values in the neighbourhood started at a million dollars, but were mostly up. *Very* up.

After all, this was Beverly Hills, and inside the Spanish-style house slept the very newest kids on the block.

*

Sixteen-year-old Brandon Walsh, his face buried in a pillow, was dreaming about his new life. He wasn't dreaming about his new home or about all the boxes he would still have to unpack in his crowded and already messy bedroom. He wasn't even dreaming about his new school, prestigious West Beverly High, or about all the new friends he would make.

In his dream he stood on a white sandy beach. Blue waves sparkling with reflected sunlight rolled lazily on shore. Walking – no, *strutting* – towards him was the perfect California blonde in the tiniest of white bikinis. She was all tanned skin and long legs and sun-bleached hair blown by the warm wind.

She smiled at him, showing her perfect teeth, moving towards him in slow motion, as lithe as a cat. Her arms reached out for him . . .

Brandon hugged the pillow, murmuring blissfully in his sleep. Rudely, the radio alarm went off.

'*Kirrrrr* . . .' Static filled the bedroom. The eyes of the moulded-plastic dragon's head Brandon had nailed to the wall flashed red. '*Wake up!*' the dragon's head intoned in its mechanical voice, '*Wake up!*'

Eyes still tightly shut, covers pulled up to his chin, Brandon flailed out, stabbing at the alarm's Off button. The radio was still tuned to a Minneapolis station, he realized in his dreamy daze, fumbling for the dial and locking in some early morning rock 'n' roll.

'. . . *That was* She Drives Me Crazy, *the Fine Young Cannibals, and this is KLOS, and it's the first day of school! So let's do it, all you fine young scholars out there! Wake me, shake me! If that didn't wake you up, boys 'n' girls, here's the news:*

'*Temperatures plummetted to record lows in the Midwest! Minneapolis reported a minus thirty! That's thirty below, can ya dig it? We're talkin' serious ice! Right here, in El Lay, it's sixty-five degrees, heading for a high of . . . You got it: sixty-five degrees! Another perfect day in paradise! . . .*'

Brandon groaned into his pillow. *First day of school. Strange city. New house. No friends* ... His eyes fluttered closed. 'I'm psyched,' he groaned.

*

Brandon's twin sister wasn't exactly buried in clothes, but she was getting there. Skirts and blouses, jackets and sweaters were strewn all about her on the floor of her new bedroom, which was separated from her brother's by a shared bathroom.

Pert Brenda Walsh moved around the cluttered room to the beat of a Steve Winwood song, trying on one outfit after another, checking herself in the mirror before rejecting each with a disgusted little pout. The piles of clothing on the floor kept growing larger.

She picked up a cardboard box near her bed, upended it and shook the contents out on the floor. Sweaters spilled everywhere. Brenda threw the empty carton on top of the other cardboard discards, a stack that reached almost to the ceiling in one corner of the bedroom.

Frustrated, Brenda put her hands on her hips and surveyed the wreckage. 'First day at a new school,' she muttered, 'and I've got nothing to wear.'

*

The day was getting off to a rocky start in her parents' bathroom, too. For one thing, Cindy and Jim Walsh kept bumping into each other as they tried to dress, navigate in the new space – all shiny chrome and freshly laid tiles – and find their things in the unfamiliar drawers and cabinets.

'Can't find my hairbrush,' Jim said irritably.

Cindy was combing her off-blonde shag. She eyed her

balding husband in the still foggy bathroom mirror and thought, *It's not as if you actually need it, dear*, but all she said was, 'Here, dear, you can use mine.'

'Thanks.' Jim Walsh, wearing a crisp white shirt and a paisley tie, eyed the hot-water faucet balefully. 'I think it's finally warming up.'

'The middle of a drought and we have to run the water for five minutes,' Cindy said distractedly, appraising herself in the mirror: Baggy sweatshirt, tight jeans; a day of house-organizing ahead of her while her husband went off to his new office and the kids went off to their new school. *Not bad for a 42-year-old*, she thought as she gazed at her reflection. 'Just try getting a glass of water in one of these fancy restaurants here and it's a major production,' she added.

'You don't want to drink the tap water in L.A. anyway,' her husband said. 'Tastes like somebody died in it. Designer water might be an affectation back in the Twin Cities, but out here you have to buy it in self-defence.'

'That's right,' Cindy agreed, walking out into the hallway, where she promptly bumped into Brenda, who was grappling with an armload of clothes and seemed, even for her, to be in an unusually frenzied state.

She looked up at her mother with a pleading expression. 'Why don't we just go shopping today, and I'll go to school tomorrow? First impressions are incredibly important, especially in Beverly Hills.'

Cindy laid a comforting hand on her daughter's shoulder. 'You're going to make a wonderful impression, dear.'

But Brenda, in a classic A-line pink shirt and a matching cardigan sweater, was certain she was heading for a fashion disaster. 'But Mom, everybody here looks like they stepped out of a music video. I don't even have the right hair.'

Seeing she wasn't even going to get sympathy, Brenda shoved the clothes into her mother's arms and stomped off to her brother's room, just as her father, shrugging into his suit jacket, joined Cindy in the hall.

'What's wrong?' he asked.

Cindy sighed. 'Your daughter has frock shock,' she said.

*

Brandon was just getting back to the good part of his dream, when his sister tickled him awake.

'Hey, cut that out, Bren!' he muttered, his face still buried in his pillow.

In reply, she yanked the sheet off him. 'You're gonna make us late, Brandon! Out of there. C'mon. Up! Up!'

Brandon yawned. 'Give me one good reason.'

Brenda sat down on the edge of the bed. 'Because you gotta help me pick out something to wear,' she said primly.

Brandon rolled over to look at her. He brushed a wave of hair out of his sleepy eyes. 'What difference does it make? We're just going to school.'

He made a grab for the sheet, but she held it out of his reach.

'Brandon!' She stood up, a school-marmish look on her face, and Brandon knew he was going to get a lecture. 'I know you were Mister Popularity at home, but *I'm* not going to miss Minneapolis.' She took a deep breath, her eyes narrowed with determination. 'Nobody knows me here. I can be anybody. I could be *somebody*. I can be somebody else.'

Brandon sat up. 'What? Homecoming queen?' he scoffed.

A look of such devastation clouded Brenda's features

that her brother hurriedly reassured her. 'Well, why not? You're cute enough.'

Instantly, she brightened. '*Really*? Are you serious?'

Brandon looked surprised.

'No, I mean it,' she continued in a rush, 'because, you know, you've never said that before . . . Do you *really* think I'm cute?'

'C'mon Bren, don't you look in the mirror? Yeah, you're cute.'

She smiled, made radiant, Brandon noticed, by his off-hand compliment. *I think I'm actually beginning to understand girls*, he thought, saying to her, 'You're just too serious is all.'

'I'm gonna fix *that*,' she said in a no-nonsense tone, crossing to the bathroom that separated their two bedrooms.

Brandon frowned. 'Hey, Bren,' he called after her, 'what about that weird black tee shirt you wore to Denise Baum's Fourth of July party? That was pretty cool.'

*

Cindy had already set out breakfast for her family in the little kitchen alcove, and now she was standing at the sink unpacking the good silver, while her husband ate.

'Ugh!' Jim Walsh set down his glass of orange juice, giving it a look of distaste as if he'd found a bug floating in it. 'The orange juice still has lumps in it,' he declared.

'The juicer isn't unpacked yet,' Cindy replied curtly, in a voice that plainly said, *Watch it, buddy*.

Jim took the hint. 'That's just an observation,' he said quickly, 'not a complaint.'

'Of course, dear.' Cindy's look mixed fondness and irritation. 'How come all *my* observations are complaints, and all *your* complaints are just observations?'

Jim looked puzzled. 'Izzat true?'

Cindy laughed affectionately and sat down across from him at the table. 'Kinda. Yeah.' She looked around the still unfamiliar kitchen. 'I just can't figure out why this house cost twice as much as we got for ours back in Minneapolis. We had a great house there, too.'

'We're paying for the address,' Jim replied thoughtfully, 'and for the schools.' He pointed out the window. 'And for that orange tree.'

'I tried one.' She screwed up her face. 'They're sour.'

Jim laughed. 'I'll be sure to mention it at our next board meeting. Right before I introduce the new software package.'

'Good, I knew you'd take care of it,' Cindy said with mock solemnity.

A minute later, when Brandon wandered in wearing his usual faded jeans and grey tee shirt, he found his parents kissing by the sink. Guiltily, they pulled apart.

'Jeez, you guys, willya cut it out?' But inside, secretly, Brandon was pleased.

'Where's Brenda?' his mother asked quickly.

'An hour in front of the mirror and she's still changing her clothes.' Brandon shrugged. 'Where's the toaster?'

His mother dug into one of the boxes and came up with the toaster. 'Here you go, dear,' she said.

His father cleared his throat and adjusted his tie. 'Keep an eye out for her today,' he said gruffly.

'Yeah? Who's looking out for me?' Brandon asked casually, taking an English muffin out of the freezer.

'I don't have to worry about you,' his father replied.

'Yeah, right,' Brandon said as his sister came in, still wearing the pink outfit.

'Popularity,' Brenda declared, 'doesn't transfer like your grade-point average.'

CHAPTER TWO

Brandon was behind the wheel of the battered '83 Honda Accord that he shared with his sister, and Brenda was in the seat next to him. They were heading South.

'Hey, where you going, Brandon? West Beverly's over that way.' She pointed towards the high-rise glass-and-steel towers of Century City.

'We got a coupla minutes,' Brandon said. 'Thought we'd take the long way, do some sight-seeing.'

They passed the Beverly Hills Hotel, the great pink monument to Hollywood's Golden Age, perched on a rise overlooking Sunset, then cruised down Rodeo Drive, Beverly Hills' shopping mecca.

Cartier. Bijan. Giorgio's. Gucci. Vidal Sassoon. The Rodeo Collection . . .

Passing in front of Van Cleef, Brandon thought he saw the girl in his dream, the perfect blonde, in a spandex minidress, a surfboard under one arm . . .

'So this is Rodeo,' Brandon said, pronouncing the street's name the way he would a cowboy show.

Brenda looked at him askance. 'Not Roh-dee-oh,' she corrected. 'Roh-*day*-oh.'

Brandon hung a right on Wilshire, across from the Regency Wilshire's ornate, flag-draped facade. They passed Nieman-Marcus, the Beverly Hills Cafe . . . He turned left, then right. They pulled up, for the first time, in front of sprawling West Beverly High . . . And simultaneously, both their mouths dropped open.

'Willya look at that.' Brandon gawked, in total awe.

Pulling into the parking lot that flanked the main building they found the most incredible array of cars Brandon had ever seen – Jaguars, Mercedes, BMWs, Porsches and Corvettes by the score; restored classics like the '57 Chevy ragtop just ahead of them and enough Jeeps to mount a good-sized desert assault.

'It's like the auto show Dad took us to when we were kids,' Brenda said.

'Only this is for real.'

Brenda glanced at her awestruck brother, then back at the cars. 'I think we're gonna need a raise in our allowance,' she said.

*

Brenda and Brandon had been brought up by their parents to have 'solid,' 'good' values – the down-to-earth values of their native Midwest – but in a very real way Brenda was right to be concerned with 'superficial' values and appearances at their new school, for they were what counted at West Beverly High.

Take Steve Sanders, for instance, who was driving his jet-black Corvette convertible through the parking lot, looking for just the right space. Tall, blond, blue-eyed, he looked more or less like some Greek statue. Not only that, his Mom was tall, blonde and blue-eyed, as well as rich and famous. Samantha Sanders was a TV star, 'America's Sweetheart,' in fact, and her series was number one in the ratings. But he didn't have it all – not anymore anyway.

He'd been ditched by the most beautiful girl in school . . . and everyone knew it. He spotted her, two aisles away:

Kelly Taylor in her new red Beemer convertible, West Beverly's self-described Credit Card Queen. 'And the biggest bitch in school,' Steve muttered to himself, heading for the space next to her, 'but I love her anyway.'

He was hardly the only one. In fact, for fourteen-year-old freshman David Silver, being driven to *his* first day at West Beverly High by his mother in her silver Jag, it was love at first sight.

He'd just tuned in the school radio station, KWBH – *'comin' at ya with over five-hundred, nasty-jammin', body-slammin' watts'* – when he glimpsed her driving past, her long straight blonde hair whipping in the wind.

David's eyes went wide. His voice, not quite under his control yet, went up an octave. 'I love this place!' he squeaked.

Kelly eased her BMW into a parking space just as a black 'vette whipped around the Silvers' Jag and swung in next to her.

She looked down her pert and perfect nose at last year's boyfriend.

'You got your licence,' he said, stating the obvious as usual.

'Hi, Steve,' she said coolly.

'Where were you all summer? I tried calling you – like, three-hundred times.' He stared at her, amazement gradually spreading across his face. 'You got a nose job!'

'Yeah,' she admitted, a defensive tinge in her voice. 'Yeah, I did.'

He stepped out of the car, unable to take his eyes off her. 'You look . . . you look *really good.*'

Kelly smiled. She turned so he could see her profile. 'Big improvement, huh?'

'I'd say they took about a foot.'

'Humpf! Now I'm remembering why I broke up with you.'

'*You* broke up with *me*? Yah, right!' Steve hopped back in the 'vette and revved the engine. 'Get real! Don't forget, I'm the one who taught you how to work a clutch.'

'I drive an automatic, thank you very much.'

'Figures.' Steve put into reverse and popped the clutch.

As he screeched away, he narrowly missed another freshman, by the name of Scott, a blond kid with a permanently goggle-eyed expression, who was wearing a backwards Lakers cap and a Surf Naked tee shirt.

Jumping out of the way, Scott bumped into the car behind him, setting off its alarm.

*

Compared to the students' parking lot, the teachers' lot looked like the L.A. Wrecking Yards. Mister Ridley, the nerdy, balding Chemistry teacher, got out of his dented Chevy Nova and steeled himself for the start of another year.

The clap on the back startled him; he thought the harassment was starting already, but it was only Jack Clayton, the Vice Principal.

'Hello there, Arthur. Nice summer?' Typically, Clayton didn't seem to have a care in the world.

Perpetually harried Mister Ridley forced a smile. 'Oh, yes. I discovered a wonderfully rare recording of the

Leningrad Philharmonic playing Prokofiev. Astonishing, really. You must let me play it for you sometime.'

'Sure thing, Arthur. Right after you join the West Beverly High Mountain Bike Club on one of our infamous Sunday morning road trips.'

Arthur Ridley was astonished. 'Isn't seven hours a day with these kids enough for you, Jack?'

The Vice Principal actually stopped to think about it. 'I don't know, Arthur . . . You know, I actually like the little suckers.'

*

Appearances weren't all that counted for *everyone* at West Beverly High. They weren't all that counted for Andrea Zuckerman.

But then Andrea wasn't your typical too-hip West Beverly student. For one thing, she didn't arrive for classes in a top-of-the-line sports car. In fact, she didn't arrive in a car at all.

Andrea Zuckerman took the bus. She disembarked a block from the school campus, getting off with five Hispanic maids, who helped her practise her Spanish on the long ride and all of whom she considered her friends.

Andrea was pretty, even her metal-rim glasses couldn't hide that. She had big, luminous, intense eyes. But she wasn't hip. Not hardly. However, she was *functional*, and she took pride in it. Everything from her nylon backpack to her sensible shoes was built to last.

And she was ambitious. Andrea knew West Beverly for what it was. She'd sacrificed to get there, and she intended to make good use of her opportunity. She took a deep breath and, with great determination, headed towards West Beverly High.

Chapter Three

Brenda and Brandon felt like two refugees just arrived in a foreign country as they picked their way shoulder-to-shoulder through the crowded hallway.

'Look for me at lunch,' Brenda whispered, eyeing the designer outfit of each girl they passed.

'Sure,' said Brandon, who was eyeing each girl they passed as well.

'I don't want to look like some geek without any friends,' Brenda hissed.

'Great,' Brandon sighed. 'Together we'll look like two geeks without any friends.'

Brenda shot him a sharp look.

'Joke, okay?' Brandon said quickly.

As they passed a row of closed doors, Brenda glanced down at a piece of paper in her hand. Brandon, oblivious to everything but the two blondes in miniskirts going in the other direction, kept walking until he was brought up short by Brenda, who had grabbed him by the sleeve.

She pointed to a nameplate next to one of the doors

that read, *JACK CLAYTON, VICE PRINCIPAL*. 'We're supposed to check in here,' Brenda said.

*

All over West Beverly, new kids were scrambling to find their first class before the final bell rang. As he rounded a corner, David Singer bumped into his old buddy Scott.

'Hey, Scott, how's it going?'

Scott looked around anxiously and adjusted the Lakers cap on his head. 'I can't find my locker, man. Fifteen thirty-three. Man, this place is *huge*! Like, five times as big as junior high.'

'Yeah,' David agreed, spotting Kelly entering a classroom at the other end of the hall, 'even the steps are bigger. But the babes are outrageous!'

*

Jack Clayton didn't look like the stereotypical Vice Principal. He was in his early thirties, handsome and easy-going; he projected a sympathetic interest in the two new students sitting across the wide expanse of desk, not a stern and distant authoritarianism.

He glanced down at the transcripts in front of him. 'Let's see: Brandon Walsh . . . Swim team . . . Sports Editor of your school paper . . . All-State Cross Country . . . and you still managed to keep a three-eight grade-point.'

He turned to the second transcript. 'Brenda Walsh . . . Drama Club . . . Student Council . . . almost a straight-A average.'

'I help her with her homework,' Brandon quipped.

Brenda shot him a look, but the Vice Principal just chuckled.

'You're both used to doing well,' he said. 'You're

both achievers. And I don't want to diminish your accomplishments, guys, but I don't want to kid you either. West Beverly is *tough*. The kids are very competitive.'

'And we're not in Minneapolis anymore,' Brandon cut in.

Brenda shot him another look, but Vice Principal Clayton didn't seem bothered. He was savvy enough to know this was Brandon's way of dealing with nervousness.

'This is one of the top five high schools in the country,' he resumed smoothly, 'and we expect a lot from our students. In some of your classes, you may have to do some catching up. You'll probably have more hours of homework than at your old school. So I want you to keep me posted on how it's going, and if you run into any problems – academic, any kind – come talk to me. It's what I'm here for.'

He stood and shook their hands. 'You're both going to do great. I'm glad to have you here. Now get going. I don't want you to be late to your first class.'

As Vice Principal Clayton ushered them out the door, they passed his secretary, who had in tow an Ozzy Osbourne lookalike, dressed all in black leather.

'Mister Clayton,' she was saying as they left, 'would you please explain to this young man our new restrictions on leather this year.'

*

Mister Ridley, in an immaculate white lab coat, surveyed the first class of the first day of the new school year. The little darlings, two to each lab table, looked like they didn't want to be studying Chemistry anymore than he wanted to be teaching it, he thought.

There were only a few empty seats left when a hostile-looking overweight girl, packed into a wildly inappropriate designer minidress, entered the back of the room.

There seemed to be one in every class, the Chemistry teacher thought sadly, some poor creature who didn't nearly measure up to the school's outrageous standards of beauty, and was therefore totally unpopular and ostracized, which made her more angry and hostile, which in turn made her more unpopular.

'Choose your seat carefully,' Mister Ridley said pointedly. 'The person sitting next to you will be your lab partner for the rest of the semester.'

Like some horror movie monster stalking the fair damsel, the overweight girl headed unerringly for Kelly Taylor and the empty seat at her table.

Kelly didn't see her until the massive shadow blotted out the fluorescent light. And like any distressed damsel, she flinched.

'Sorry,' she said sweetly, 'it's taken.'

The girl scowled. 'By who?'

Kelly's sweet smile grew thinner as it froze into place; her eyes scanned the room frantically. 'There! That girl.' One manicured finger stabbed in the direction of Brenda, late and frazzled, who was just slipping into the back of the room.

The overweight girl glared suspiciously at Brenda as Kelly waved her over.

'Hi! Over here,' Kelly called out.

Brenda just looked confused.

'C'mon, I saved you a seat.'

Brenda pointed at herself questioningly. Kelly nodded an emphatic yes. As Brenda eased into the empty seat, the overweight girl moved on.

'Thanks,' Brenda said, 'but I think you're confusing me with somebody else.'

'That's okay,' Kelly replied breezily. 'I'm being friendly.'

'Oh.' It wasn't quite what Brenda had expected on her first day of school. 'Well, thanks. I'm Brenda.'

'I'm Kelly.'

'Hi.'

As always, Kelly had her eye fixed firmly on whatever would make her own life easier. 'Are you smart?' she asked.

'Well, sort of,' Brenda hedged.

'This class is a real bitch,' Kelly declared. 'I need all the help I can get.'

Chapter Four

Brandon, too, was late for his first class, Spanish II, and when he came through the door, thirty pairs of eyes gave him the once-over.

Self-consciously, he made his way down the narrow aisles, searching for an empty seat. He found one, between a pretty brunette wearing metal-rim glasses and a blond, jockish-looking guy – Andrea Zuckerman and Steve Sanders.

Their teacher was Miss Montes De La Roca, a pretty, buxom woman with a sexy gap between her teeth.

She wrote her name on the blackboard, then turned to the students. Speaking entirely in lilting Spanish, she said, '*I am Miss De La Roca, and this is Spanish II. We will be conducting all of this year's class entirely in Spanish. No English will be permitted in class? Do you all understand?*'

Thirty faces stared blankly back at her.

Still speaking in Spanish, she added. '*If you understand, please raise your hand.*'

The faces continued to stare.

Steve leaned in close to Brandon and whispered. 'How bogus. The lady gets paid for speaking her mother tongue.'

'*Does anyone understand me?*' Miss Montes asked again in Spanish.

Only Andrea Zuckerman's hand went up. Miss Montes smiled.

A few students, among them Steve Sanders, turned and shot Andrea dirty looks. Then, just to be on the safe side, they raised their hands too. In a flash, every student in the classroom had a hand in the air.

'Es impresionate,' Miss Montes said with just a trace of irony. Then, catching Andrea's eye, she added, 'Muchos gracias.'

Andrea shrugged. 'No importa,' she replied.

*

It was a working newsroom in miniature, abuzz with frenzy and intense concentration, with student reporters at computer terminals, working their stories.

He recognized the pretty girl with glasses from his Spanish class. She was seated behind one of the desks, proofing copy.

'Hola,' Brandon said to her.

Andrea looked up without answering. She was one girl who wasn't easily charmed.

'We're in Spanish together,' Brandon said. 'I'm Brandon.'

'Hola,' Andrea said at last.

Brandon looked around. 'I'm looking for the editor,' he said, managing to sound more self-important than he'd intended. 'Andrea Zuckerman, do you know her?'

Andrea checked him out. 'You found her,' she replied.

Brandon managed not to look too surprised. He

pulled up a chair next to her. 'I want to write for the paper,' he said, fixing her with an intense look.

Andrea arched an eyebrow. 'Can you write?'

'I was the sports editor at my old school in Minneapolis.'

'Great,' Andrea said lightly. 'Now which would you rather cover – toxic waste disposal in our chemistry labs or the girls' water polo match against Beverly High?'

Brandon didn't even need a tenth of a second to consider the question. 'We didn't have a girls' water polo team back in Minneapolis, so I'll go for the new experience. What time's the game?'

Andrea shot him a disgusted, you-men-are-all-alike look. 'You *definitely* failed my test.'

'Huh? . . . I don't get it.'

'It's simple,' said Andrea, in that tone women reserve for young children, mental defectives and un-evolved men. 'Whenever a guy wants to work for the paper, I ask him, "Do you want to cover the girls' polo match, or do you want to do the toxic waste story?" Not one guy has *ever* chosen the toxic waste story . . . Now, just *why* is that, Brandon?'

Brandon had a ready answer. 'Human nature.'

'Hah! . . . No offence, but this is the top-ranked high school paper in the whole country, and I intend to keep it that way.' Andrea said acidly. 'So put aside your dreams of editing the swimsuit issue of *Sports Illustrated*. We're talking about long hours, *major* deadlines, total commitment . . . Still interested?'

Andrea expected hostility (she courted it, after all), she expected defensiveness, she was even ready for fawning insincerity. What she didn't expect was Brandon's huge grin.

'Wow, you are *intense*.'

Despite herself, she smiled back. 'I know,' she

admitted sheepishly. 'But that's what it takes to do what we do around here. So, if you don't want to make the sacrifices, I'll totally understand.'

Abruptly, Brandon stood. 'I guess I should start by interviewing the janitor.'

Andrea corrected him automatically. 'Custodial engineer.'

Brandon nodded, shrugged – an implicit acknowledgement that he had a lot to learn. He turned towards the door.

'Brandon,' she called after him.

He stopped with his hand on the knob and looked back at her.

Andrea Zuckerman smiled warmly, and for just that moment her no-nonsense persona dissolved. 'Nice meeting you,' she said.

The flash of radiance cut clean through Brandon's own guard. He grinned crookedly back. 'Uh . . . yeah. Nice meeting you too.'

*

Lunch hour alfresco at West Beverly High. Not like snowbound Minneapolis, Brandon thought, carrying his lunch tray and hunting for a place at the outdoor tables where he could sit down. Cliques were cliques everywhere though, and Brandon could sense the tight little knots of friends, each group at its own table, tensing as the stranger walked by.

At last, Brandon spotted an empty seat at a table of fashionably dressed kids (as if there were any other kind at West Beverly, Brandon thought), who seemed engaged in carefree, animated, chattering conversation.

Brandon stopped, listening unobtrusively for a moment, trying to catch the gist of the conversation.

'Any of you guys seen Lauren yet?' a girl was saying. 'You won't believe this, but she fell in love with Adam Beauregard over summer vacation.'

The boy across from her seemed shocked by the revelation. 'No way! That geek? She's way too cute for *him*.'

'He's been working out,' the girl replied, as if confiding a great truth.

Brandon sat down in the empty place next to them. The girl glanced over at him, but she seemed to look right through him. 'C'mon,' she said suddenly, 'we gotta get to class.'

And without missing a beat, they all stood, leaving Brandon alone.

*

Kelly and Brenda, each sipping a diet Coke, weaved their way through the crowded lunch-hour picnic tables. Like visiting royalty, Kelly favoured selected groups of her subjects with a casual little wave.

'It's a good thing you met me when you did,' Kelly breezily informed her newest friend. 'West Beverly isn't like other schools. Kids here are richer. Some of their parents are celebs. So, it's definitely *not* your normal high school.

'Socially, it's really intense. You make one false move and you're history. I mean, if people saw you eating lunch alone today like that guy over there . . .'

Brenda followed Kelly's haughty gaze: *Brandon!* She was talking about Brandon, sitting at a distant table away from the centre of action, all alone. Adroitly, she manoeuvred Kelly in the opposite direction before her brother could spot them.

'I had great friends at my old school,' Brenda said quickly.

'In Minneapolis?' She said it as if she were saying 'In the stockyards?'

'Yeah,' Brenda answered defensively.

'But it's so cold there,' said Kelly. 'I could never deal with cold.'

Despite herself, Brenda was getting miffed. 'You'd get over it,' she said tonelessly, but Kelly didn't notice.

'I'd get fat,' she declared.

'Yeah, but it's great. All winter you can eat whatever you want and hide it under bulky sweaters.'

Kelly, who couldn't remember a time when she was not dieting, laughed. 'That's *definitely* not Beverly Hills. Somebody here is always throwing a pool party, it doesn't matter what time of year. So you never get a chance to really pig out.'

*

The two hapless freshmen, Scott and David, were having their own lunch-hour traumas. Balancing a large stack of books along with their lunch trays, they made their way outside.

'I can't believe we've got all this reading!' Scott whined. '*The Great Gatsby* by next week? I mean, that's an eleventh-grade book!'

'Plus Trig, History, French and Biology. It's outrageous!' David exclaimed, spotting Kelly, the blonde of his dreams. 'What's going to happen to our social lives?'

'I'm asking my mother for a tutor, is what,' Scott replied, as they passed some jock-types throwing around a football. 'If you screw up in ninth grade, you can *permanently* damage your high school GPA.'

'Hey, buddy,' one of them called out to Scott. 'Think quick!'

He threw the football. Instinctively, Scott tried to catch it. His lunch tray and the books crashed to the floor.

The football players guffawed at Scott's expense.

'Jocks!' Scott spat the word out. 'I *hate* jocks!'

But then he noticed that they'd already stopped paying attention to him. Suddenly, everybody was looking up and pointing to the sky.

'I don't believe it!' David sputtered, craning his head back. Far overhead, a small aeroplane was criss-crossing in the blue sky. It trailed a long banner, on one side of which was printed the following words:

BACK TO SHOOL JAM. FRIDAY NIGHT. 29150 SKYLINE DRIVE. BE THERE!

David was ecstatic. He punched hapless Scott, who was trying to pick up his books. 'Alright! We're there! We're there!'

Like everyone else in the lunch-hour crowd, Brenda and Kelly were looking up too.

'Wow,' said Brenda. 'That's some invitation.'

'Oh my God!' Kelly exclaimed, as the address on the flapping banner came into view. 'That's Marianne Moore's house. She's incredibly rich, but a real party girl. I hear the house is so big you need a map and a golf cart to get round it.'

'I can't believe she's inviting the whole school,' said Brenda. 'I mean, that must be eighteen-hundred people!'

The plane banked and turned, and now they could see the curt legend on the banner's other side:

NO FRESHMEN!

'Make that thirteen-hundred,' Kelly said. 'Want to go together?'

Brenda smiled. 'Sure.'

On the other side of the crowd, David and Scott spotted the same two, devastating words. It was as if the

30

plane had dropped a bomb right on them.

'Jeez,' Scott said. 'What a drag!'

But David was defiant. 'I don't care. We're still going.'

CHAPTER FIVE

The first week of school had passed in a blur of classes, homework assignments and newspaper deadlines. And now that Friday evening had finally come, Brandon was stretched out on his bed, exhausted, a book balanced on his chest.

There was a knock on the bedroom door and his father poked his head in. 'Not going to the big party?' He nodded in the direction of Brenda's room. 'Your sister's been getting ready for hours.'

'Nah. I'm beat.'

Jim Walsh looked at his son askance. 'After only a week?'

'Dad, this *is* West Beverly High.'

Jim thought that over. 'From what I've heard about West Beverly, the parties are pretty great . . . Even for the new kids.'

Brandon looked adamant, so his father shrugged and walked out, closing the door behind him.

Outside, a horn honked. Brandon closed the book, pulled himself up and went to the window. It was that

Kelly babe in her red BMW convertible, along with three other girls from her crowd. She beeped again.

As Brandon watched, his sister came out . . . escorted by their mother. Brandon groaned to himself: even back in Minneapolis that sort of thing was definitely uncool. He didn't have to see the look on his sister's face to share her embarrassment.

It was something Kelly and her friends pounced on too. 'I'd die if my mother did that to me,' one in the back seat hissed.

'Give her a break,' Kelly said over her shoulder. 'They're from out of town.'

Brenda wore a black and silver sweater, black slacks and heels; her mother was in jeans and an old work shirt of Jim's. Cindy Walsh had her arm draped casually over her daughter's shoulder as they walked around to the driver's side of the Beemer. An embarrassed smile was frozen on Brenda's face.

'This is my mom,' Brenda said. 'Mom, this is Kelly—'

'Hi, Kelly,' Cindy said.

'And this is Donna . . . and Cathy . . . and Michelle,' Brenda added, indicating each girl in turn.

The girls all chirped pleasant hellos. Cindy looked relieved: Brenda's new friends seemed decent enough, and there weren't any boys in the car.

'Nice to meet you all,' she said. 'You look like you're ready to have a good time . . . When's curfew?'

The four girls in the car looked as if they'd never even heard the word before.

'Excuse me?' Kelly said.

'See?' Brenda turned to her mother. 'I told you so.' Then she marched around the front of the car and got in.

'How about midnight, Bren?' Cindy said. Somehow, to the girls, it didn't sound like a question.

Donna giggled, and Kelly shot her a look that instantly stifled the sound.

'Twelve-thirty,' Brenda declared.

Cindy sighed. 'Twelve-fifteen,' she said firmly.

Kelly gave Brenda's mother a totally insincere smile, put the car into gear and slowly headed off.

'God, that was embarrassing!' Brenda exclaimed as they headed away from the house.

God, that was embarrassing, Brandon thought to himself upstairs, as he watched the red Beemer round the corner. He turned around, stared for a moment at the book on the bed, then grabbed his sportsjacket off a peg on the wall and headed for the door.

*

David's mother *heard* the party – blaring rock with a bass line that seemed to reverberate up the length of her spine – even before the Jag rounded the corner and she got her first glimpse of the imposing, gated Moore mansion, set on a knoll overlooking the city. Cars were parked bumper to bumper along the circular drive and up and down the street below.

'David, I'm not sure about this,' she said. 'Are the girl's parents home?'

David, sitting next to her, craned his head out the window. 'Mom would you relax? It's just a party.'

David's mother turned to Scott, wearing a blazer a size too big for him and his trademark Lakers cap, in the back seat. 'And your mother's coming to pick you boys up at eleven, right?'

Scott, wide-eyed, nodded his head up and down, too nervous even to speak.

Up ahead of them, Steve Sanders eased his Corvette into a parking place near the top of the drive.

*

Kids were streaming into the house from every direction. To Brandon, who'd parked a block-and-a-half away and was approaching the great house on foot, it seemed as if the entire school had actually turned out for the party.

He stopped at the foot of the drive and stared up at the mansion. Fairy lights hung from the trees, pinpoint spots converged on the front entrance. Candles and revolving party lights in a rainbow of primary colours illuminated the vast interior. It was quite simply the biggest house he'd ever seen.

As he trudged on the long, upward-sweeping drive, Brandon passed Steve Sanders, who was just getting out of the black 'vette. In Steve's hand was a brown paper bag.

'Hey, Steve,' Brandon said, forcing himself to be sociable. 'Hey, Brandon.'

They fell in step together, walking up the last few feet to the entrance. 'Some car,' Brandon observed, hooking a thumb at the shiny Corvette.

'We all gotta have something to live for.'

Brandon nodded towards the imposing house. 'Who *is* this girl?' he asked, dumbfounded. 'Does she have parents or what?'

Jovially, Steve slapped Brandon on the back, smiling at the new kid's naiveté. 'Welcome to West Beverly High, man.'

They reached the front door and Steve swung it open. The party may have just started, but already it was ratcheted up to overdrive. Pounding music hit Brandon in the face. Somewhere in the throbbing, strobe-raked scene that greeted them, glass broke.

Steve gave Brandon an idiot's grin. 'After you, man,' he said. And the two of them pushed their way inside.

*

CHAPTER SIX

The enormous terraced back yard of the Moore Mansion looked like the grounds of a country club, with an Olympic-sized swimming pool overlooking a double tennis court that had been converted to a dance floor. A rock band blazed from behind the baseline.

It's the ultimate party, Brandon thought, as he and Steve stepped through the French doors and looked out over the pool area. Drop-dead gorgeous girls in the skimpiest of bikinis were splashing in the pool and soaking in the nearby jacuzzi. Below them, spread out jewel-like, was all of night-time L.A.

'What's your type?' Steve asked.

Brandon looked at him uncomprehendingly.

'You know ... Blonde, brunette, short, tall, good legs, good buns ... What?'

'Yes,' Brandon replied.

Steve threw back his head and laughed. He took a big swig from his paper bag. 'My man! ... Don't let me get in your way.'

*

On the other side of the pool, Brenda, Kelly and Donna picked their way carefully through a group of carousing party animals pushing each other into the water. All around them the party swirled, ever wilder.

A drunken football jock in a rugby shirt weaved past. 'Hey, Kelly. Lookin' good,' he exclaimed, before disappearing among the revellers.

'Wow.' said Kelly, 'He's never said *that* before.'

'Okay,' Donna shot back irritably, tossing her mane of straight blonde hair, 'so it's changed your life.' Gingerly, she touched the tip of her own prominent proboscis. 'Maybe I should get mine done too.'

Kelly could tell Brenda didn't have the slightest idea what they were talking about. 'I had a deviated septum,' she explained.' Rhinoplasty, ya know?'

Donna giggled. Brenda got it. '*You* had a nose job? . . .' She took a close look. 'It's beautiful.'

Kelly was thrilled. 'It is, isn't it,' she enthused. 'Gee, I wish I'd looked like this when I was a freshman.'

Brenda was looking past her. She waved to someone on the other side of the pool.

'Who're you waving to? Kelly asked.

'My brother. Brandon.'

Kelly regarded him with an eye towards the possibilities. 'He's cute,' she mused. 'OhmyGod! . . . He's with Steve Sanders.'

'The big blond guy?' Brenda asked. 'Who's that?'

'My old boyfriend,' Kelly replied dismissively. 'And he's having a tough time getting the message that it's over. O–V–E–R.'

On the other side of the pool, Steve, too, wanted to know who Brandon was waving at. 'Who's the babe, bud?' he asked, his words beginning to slur.

'My sister.' Brandon shot him a take-care-what-you-say look.

'Looks like she's hangin' out with Kelly Taylor.'
'The blonde?'
'Yeah,' Steve said glumly.
'She's cute.'
'She's my old girlfriend.'
'So what happened?' Brandon prompted.
'I dumped her over the summer,' Steve said, and then he wandered away.

*

Timidly, David and Scott edged ever closer to the action by the pool. Scott, for whom an hour at the video arcade was a walk on the wild side, was totally terrified, but David was too agog to be scared.

'This is totally mind-blowing,' David declared. 'Another coupla hours and I bet some of these girls start taking off their tops.'

'Think so?' Just the thought came near to short-circuiting Scott's already boggled mind.

'Definitely,' David said authoritatively.

'But we're not going to be here,' Scott said quickly, taking refuge in the thought. 'My mother's coming to pick us up at eleven.'

'If I see skin, I'm staying.'

Two jocks in swimming trunks ambled by, their menacing gazes raking the two freshmen.

'Hey, dudes,' David said brightly, but they ignored him.

'I think we should go,' Scott said, a note of urgency in his reedy voice. 'I don't feel very welcome.'

'Would you relax already?' David picked up two cups of punch from a nearby bar and handed one to his nervous friend. 'Here. Have some punch or something.'

Scott downed a big gulp and . . . spat it out, coughing.

But David was too entranced to notice. Drop-jawed, wide-eyed, he was staring at Kelly Taylor, who was talking with Brenda and Donna.

David grabbed Scott's arm in a vice-like grip. He pointed at the blonde vision. 'Hey, that's her! That's the girl I was telling you about.'

Scott gulped and cleared his throat. 'Where?'

'See . . . Over there.' David pointed. 'The totally foxy blonde. I wonder if she goes for younger guys?'

One look at Kelly and Scott was convinced of the answer. But he tried to break it gently to his pal. 'I doubt it.'

'I'm gonna go stand closer to her,' David said in an awed hush.

'What about me?' It wasn't a question, it was a whining plea.

David pulled his eyes away from his vision and whipped the Lakers cap off Scott's head. 'Mingle' was all that he said.

'Sure,' Scott said to himself as David disappeared. He glanced around: nothing but drunken, six-foot-tall jocks, whose menacing glances Scott tried not to meet. He swallowed hard.

*

Brandon moved solitary through the laughing and shouting, drinking and dancing, gettin' down and partying crowd. Everyone was carefree and happy, he felt, except him. In the middle of the noisy swirl, he threw his hands up in a gesture of resignation.

'Alright.' he said to himself, 'I'm outta here.' He strode purposefully across the wide lawn, on a whim saying goodbye to people who didn't even know he existed. 'See ya later, man . . . It's been a blast . . . Later . . .'

On the edge of the party, he spotted a pretty, pale, raven-haired girl, standing alone, a drink in her hand. She looked as sad and isolated as he felt. Brandon stopped and turned back to her.

'Hey,' he said, coming up next to her.

She looked up at him.

Brandon smiled at her. 'You here by yourself?'

She nodded slowly.

'Whadya know!' Brandon tossed his head back to get an unruly strand of hair out of his eyes. 'I'm here by myself too . . .' He scanned the revellers. 'This party really sucks,' he said heatedly.

'I know,' the girl said softly.

'I mean, for somebody who doesn't know anyone.'

The raven-haired girl was surprised. 'Why don't you know anybody? I mean, do you go to Beverly or West Beverly High?'

'West Beverly,' Brandon replied, unable to keep the disdain out of his voice. 'We just moved out here.'

'Lucky you,' the girl replied, her voice dripping sarcasm.

There was something very appealing about the girl, about the mixture of tough sarcasm and her obvious vulnerability, Brandon decided. 'So, what's your story?' he asked.

Unexpectedly, she shot him a bold, seductive look. 'You're very sexy,' she said, looking him directly in the eye.

Brandon was, to say the least, taken off guard. 'Uh, thanks . . . So are you.'

'Want to dance?' she asked.

'Sure.' He held out his hand, to guide her to the dance floor.

'No . . . Right here.'

Brandon shrugged. 'Okay.' The lonely edge of the

party was as good a place as any.

She put her arms around his neck, and by some mutual, unspoken consent, they began to slow dance in sensual counterpoint to the driving rock music drifting up from the tennis courts.

'These parties are so bogus,' she whispered in his ear. 'Every year it's the same old crowd.'

'So, why did you come?'

'I didn't have any choice,' the girl replied.

That seemed puzzling. 'Why?'

Under his arms, the girl shrugged. Softly she said, 'Because it's my house.'

Brandon was stunned. 'Wait a second.' He stopped dancing and pulled away. 'This is *your* party?'

She nodded, pulling him back, even closer. 'Don't. You smell good.' She nuzzled his neck. 'What's that you're wearing?'

'I don't know.' Brandon shrugged. 'Tide.'

She laughed. Little puffs of air caressed Brandon's neck. 'What's your name?' he asked.

'Marianne . . . What's yours?'

'Brandon.'

'Hi, Brandon.'

They continued to slow dance.

'So,' began Brandon after a moment, 'isn't it kinda weird, like, not talking to people at your own party?'

Marianne rested her head on his shoulder. 'I don't know,' she said dreamily. 'My parents tell me to be social . . . God knows *they* are . . . Just 'cause I'm popular doesn't mean I have to like everybody.'

The music ended. The band announced a short break. The spell seemed broken.

Abruptly, Marianne pulled away and turned to go. 'Well . . . it was nice meeting you.'

Brandon stopped her with a light touch on her bare

arm. 'Hey, you think I could call you sometime?'

Marianne shrugged. 'Sure ... anytime,' she said, pulling a lipstick out of her pocket and writing her phone number on Brandon's forearm.

'Try not to smear it,' she said, a mischievous twinkle in her eye. And before Brandon could react, she kicked off her shoes and ran with childlike abandon towards the crowded pool.

'*Everybody into the pool!*' she yelled out at the top of her lungs.

As Brandon watched, totally captivated, she leapt onto the bandstand and began dancing with wild, sexy abandon. Everyone outside stopped to watch her uninhibited performance.

Suddenly, she yelled out again, as if commanding the crowd: '*Everybody into the pool! Right now!*'

And with that, she jumped off the bandstand and ran headlong towards the pool. Dozens of fully-dressed kids turned on their heels and raced her to be the first to jump in.

Scott, who'd found himself a quiet corner poolside to hide out until his mother arrived, looked in horror as a wave of partygoers crashed over him, throwing him and each other in the water. One after another, like chic lemmings, they plunged. All except Marianne.

She stopped abruptly at the very edge of the pool, laughing lustily at all the kids she'd duped into getting soaked. And with that, she turned grandly and marched off into the depths of the house.

CHAPTER SEVEN

At West Beverly, Steve Sanders was usually Mister Popularity – a sociable, gregarious, party-hearty kind of guy.

But not tonight, and not at *this* party. He didn't know it, but he felt just like Brandon – alone and isolated in the middle of the crowd.

He stood by himself, weaving slightly, and stared forlornly at Kelly on the other side of the lawn. Every few seconds, he took another big pull from the bottle in the paper bag.

Kelly seemed so carefree and happy, laughing and talking, with her steady girlfriend Donna and her new buddy, Brandon's sister . . . It just didn't seem fair, Steve thought drunkenly. On an impulse, he started towards them.

*

'What we've got to do,' Kelly was saying conspiratorially, 'is get ourselves some fake I.D.s.'

Brenda looked dubious.

'It's the only way to get into some clubs, meet some older guys.'

'You think *we* could pass for twenty-one?' Brenda asked.

'Definitely,' said Kelly. 'It's all attitude.'

'Uh-oh.' Donna peered over Kelly's shoulder. 'Steve's coming over here, Kelly ... and he's lookin' kinda blasted.'

It wasn't just drunkenness that was apparent in Steve's rolling gait, but belligerence too.

'Hi, Kelly,' he said, coming to a swaying stop.

'Hi.'

'So ... you wanna dance?'

'No thanks. I'm fine right here.'

Steve looked foggily in the direction of the tennis courts. 'Everybody's dancin',' he said.

Kelly fixed him with a disapproving eye. 'I said, *I don't want to dance*. Whadya want from me?'

Steve loomed over Kelly, swaying. Donna backed away a step. Brenda bit her lower lip. The tension of the moment was ominous and thick.

'Man, you are *so* cold!'

'Steve, get over it!' Kelly shot back.

'Get over it y'rself,' Steve slurred, abruptly walking away. As he staggered off, he took a long and ostentatious drag on his bottle.

'Way t'go, Kel,' Donna burbled. 'You were really strong.'

Brenda said nothing; she smiled supportively at her new friend. But watching drunken Steve Sanders making his wobbly way alone, she thought, *How sad!*

*

Steve was not only having trouble keeping his equilibrium, it was also getting harder to properly focus his eyes. Some eager little freshman with a squeaky voice seemed to be blathering something about Kelly to him.

'Huh?' said Steve, belching and squinting down.

'I said,' said David Silver, 'do you know her, man?'

'Yeah.' Steve growled, 'I know her.'

'She's hot,' David said with almost religious fervour.

Steve shot the little freshman a disgusted look. 'She's the biggest bitch at West Beverly High! And I should know . . . I went out with her for a year.'

David couldn't believe it. 'What . . . what happened?'

'I dumped her,' Steve snarled. 'She's lousy in bed and she's got a nasty personality.'

'I could live with that,' David said.

Steve peered drunkenly down at him. 'Who are you anyway?'

David automatically extended his hand. 'David Silver.'

Steve shook it, reluctantly. 'Shteve Sanders,' he slurred.

'Wait a minute.' David had just heard the only thing that could drive the vision of Kelly, 'lousy in bed' or not, out of his head. 'Your mom . . . she's not . . .'

Steve nodded solemnly.

David just gaped. 'Samantha Sanders? The mom in *Hartley House*?'

Again, Steve just nodded.

'OhmyGod! I don't believe it!' David gushed. 'I grew up watching that show . . . in re-runs. Five years on Channel Four at seven-thirty. Then it moved to Channel Seven at Six. Then for a couple of years it was on *twice* a day, at nine in the morning and five-thirty—'

'Alright, alright.' Annoyed, Steve cut him off. 'I get the point.'

But David was too revved up to stop. 'I don't believe

it! I really *love* your mom. She's like ... the *perfect mom.*'

Steve snorted derisively. 'I hate to break your heart, kid, but my mom's not the perfect mom.' Taking another swig, he pointed towards Kelly. 'And *that* ain't the perfect girl.' And then he staggered off, disappearing into the crowd, leaving David gaping, until ...

He looked down at his watch. 'Oh, no!' It was eleven-oh-five!

'Scott! Scott!' He raced off down the side of the pool in search of his friend.

*

Steve was by himself on the dance floor, doing a staggering little dance. The band had stopped playing and the party was breaking up. Somebody grabbed him by the elbow.

'Hey, Sanders, you're plastered. Somebody driving you home?'

Steve recognized the face, just. He shoved at the vaguely familiar kid. 'Go 'way! Don' worry 'bout me.'

*

David was frantic. The fabulous party was breaking up and people were leaving in droves. He dashed around the top of the steeply down-sloping driveway grabbing kids he didn't know at random, like a drowning man grabbing at life preservers.

'Hey, have you seen this kid, kinda skinny, probably wet? ...'

A sophomore girl shrugged free of his grasp. 'Get lost, freak,' she said.

'Yeah, sure. Right. Thanks for your help.' David

slumped dejectedly against the side of a parked car. 'You ditched me, you dork!' he said bitterly to himself.

He jumped at the sounds of a scuffle behind him. A couple of senior guys had Steve Sanders pinned to the ground; a third was trying to get into his pockets to get his car keys.

Steve struggled free, but not before one of the seniors had snatched the keys.

'Got 'em,' he called out triumphantly as Steve made a drunken grab for them. 'Whoa. You're not driving, dude. You're trashed, my man.'

In an instant of drunken lucidity, Steve saw David out of the corner of his eye. 'He'll drive me home,' he said, wagging a finger in David's approximate direction. 'He's a ol' friend.'

'Hey, wait. I don't—' David started to protest, but the senior shrugged and threw him the keys.

The soused finger wagged in the direction of a shiny black Corvette. 'There's my car,' Steve burbled.

'OhmyGod!' David said under his breath, as two of the seniors grabbed Steve under the arms and dumped him in the sports car's passenger seat. Before David could make his mind up to confess that he didn't have his driver's licence yet, the samaritans had strolled nonchalantly away.

Gingerly, David got behind the wheel of the 'vette. Next to him, Steve was on the verge of nodding out.

'Uh, Steve, uh, where do you live, man?'

'Donheny Road,' Steve mumbled. 'Forty-two-oh-three.'

Carefully, like a safecracker handling nitroglycerin, David turned the key in the ignition. The powerful engine roared to life.

'Say, Steve?'

'Yeah, li'l pal?'

'I don't know if I can do this.'

'Sure ya can. Jus' put it in gear an' drive away,' Steve said, gesturing grandly.

'There's one thing I gotta tell you before we get going.'

Steve was barely conscious. 'Huhhhh?'

David turned to him nervously. 'I don't have my licence. Is that a problem for you?'

Steve's eyes fluttered open. Disconcertingly, he began to laugh hysterically. David's admission seemed to be the funniest thing he'd ever heard.

David gulped. 'Guess not,' he said, putting the car into gear and lurching down the driveway and onto the now-deserted road.

Steve, laughing harder than ever, slipped a Guns 'n' Roses CD in the 'vette's player, and as Axl Rose began to sing *Knockin' On Heaven's Door*, David punched it into second.

The car shot forward and Scott's Laker's cap went flying off David's head, landing in the back seat.

*

As it was every weekend, Sunset Boulevard was bumper-to-bumper with cruising cars. David drove with the top down and windows up, manoeuvring as carefully as a man making his way past broken glass.

Steve stirred, rolled down his window and hung his head and half his torso out the car. 'I need air, man . . .'

'Hey, no! Don't do that!' David took one hand off the wheel and pulled Steve back inside . . . just as the car in front of him stopped for a light.

David hit the brakes. The car screeched to a halt inches behind the other auto's rear bumper. Steve was thrown forward, knocking his head against the dashboard. He began laughing again. 'Hey! Learn how to drive,' he said.

David's nerves were about to snap. 'I'm doing better than *you* could, and I don't even know *how* . . .

'I don't get it. How could you own a rad car like this and ever even *think* about driving drunk?'

'But I'm *not* driving,' Steve replied with impeccable inebriated logic. '*You're* driving.'

'Jeez!' David turned away in disgust and found himself staring wide-eyed into the red BMW convertible that had pulled up next to them at the light. The Beemer was postively *packed* with beautiful girls, but at the wheel was *the* girl of his hyperactive dreams . . . *Kelly Taylor*!

Nervously feigning nonchalance, he gave a twitchy little wave. 'How's it goin', babe?'

Kelly could *not* believe what she was seeing. 'OhmyGod!' Brenda and Donna and the other girls crowded into the BMW craned their heads to look.

David nodded and smiled and winked suavely. It felt *soooo* cool!

'Steve! Steve!' Donna yelled, leaning across Brenda, trying to get his attention. 'There's some geek driving your car!'

David's preening face dropped about a mile. The light turned green and the girls, giggling at his expense, pulled smoothly away. Behind him, an impatient cruiser honked and flashed his lights. Crestfallen, David lurched into traffic.

He peered into the rearview mirror . . . and thought he'd swoon: a police car was right behind the Corvette!

Instinctively, David punched the semi-comatose Steve in the arm. 'Cops!' he hissed. 'There's a cop behind us! Sit up! Look normal!'

The police black-and-white edged up alongside them.

One of the cops was giving the Corvette the once-over.

David forced his panicked features into a broad smile and nodded at the policeman in greeting. Next to him, Steve was sitting up, ramrod straight, a lopsided grin frozen on his face. For a sickening moment, David was certain they were going to be pulled over. But instead, the cop returned his nod and the police car pulled away.

*

Somehow, they'd made it. The Corvette stopped on a slight incline, at the top of the Sanders' drive. David turned off the engine and handed Steve the keys.

Grinning idiotically, Steve hauled himself out of the car and headed into a large ranch-style house. 'Thanks, bud,' he called out groggily. 'I'll remember you for this.'

'No problem,' David said, getting out. He suddenly felt weak-kneed and leaned against the front of the 'vette. 'Catch you later!' But Steve was already inside . . .

A curious sensation washed over the emotionally drained freshman. For a second he felt drunk, then thought, *Maybe it's an earthquake!* Then . . .

The Corvette was rolling backwards, quickly picking up speed! David watched in horror as it rolled down the drive, across the street and . . . smashed into a parked Mercedes.

'OhmyGod, no!'

Lights were going on in a neighbour's house. Torn by doubt, he stood for a second rooted to the spot. Then finally . . . David ran!

In Chemistry class, Mister Ridley was droning on and on and on, in a language that might almost have been Spanish.

Brenda and Kelly were huddled together over a single textbook, apparently hanging on every word. However . . .

Inside the textbook was Brenda's driver's licence. Kelly — in her practised, expensively manicured hand — was busily altering the birthdate.

'This is going to be great,' Kelly enthused.

Brenda reached for it. 'Lemme see.'

'Not yet.' Kelly covered it protectively with one hand. 'You're gonna be able to get into any club in town. I am such an artiste.'

Suddenly, the droning stopped. 'Excuse me. Ladies in the back of the room . . .'

Brenda looked up, terrified.

'I'm not in the habit of lecturing pre-schoolers. So either have the courtesy to pay attention, or get out of my class. Now.'

Brenda was aghast. She couldn't remember the last time she'd been reprimanded in a class. But Kelly took it in her stride. 'I'll show you at lunch,' she whispered, favouring Mister Ridley with her most sincere smile.

*

'He's going to kill me. I'm just waiting to die.'

David and Scott, their nylon backpacks weighted down with books, were wandering the lunch-hour grounds.

David was in disguise — a porkpie hat and wraparound shades. Scott looked the way he always did, minus, of course, his treasured Lakers cap.

'I can't believe you actually drove his 'vette. Where'd you learn how to drive?'

'My dad. He lets me drive *his* 'vette on weekends. That's what happens when your parents are divorced. Your dad lets you do incredibly stupid things because he only sees you on weekends.'

Behind the wraparounds, David's eyes were constantly scanning from side-to-side, as if he were some spy straight out of *Mad* magazine. So paranoid was he that when he and Scott walked right past the picnic table where Brenda, Kelly and Donna were sitting, he didn't even notice the girl of his dreams.

The three girls' eyes were all focused on the same spot: Brenda's newly forged driver's licence.

Brenda was in awe. 'Wow! Nineteenth sixty-nine. Do you think anybody would really believe it, really believe that I'm that old?'

Kelly was all professional reassurance. 'First of all, nobody here knows what a Minnesota driver's licence even looks like,' she pointed out. 'And anyway, I think it really depends on whether the doorman thinks you're cute.'

Brenda studied it carefully. 'I don't know . . .'

Kelly took umbrage; after all, she did do the highest-quality work.

'It looks great, it really does,' Brenda said quickly. 'It's just that . . . it's against the law. I guess I've never broken a law before.' Even to herself, she sounded like such a goody-goody. 'God, I'm such a case!'

Donna, who was the voice of what passed for normality at West Beverly, chimed in: 'The worst that can happen is they don't let you in.'

Brenda took a deep breath. She remembered what she's promised herself before the first day of school: No more Miss Serious! No more Miss Practicality! 'So when do we test this out? she asked bravely.

'Saturday night,' Kelly said. 'The Blue Iguana. Are we there?'

'Definitely!' said Brenda, with a certainty she didn't entirely feel.

*

His twin sister didn't seem to be having any trouble making friends, Brandon noticed; in fact, she was hanging out all the time with Kelly and what seemed to be the tightest, most exclusive little clique in all of West Beverly.

Brandon gazed around the maze of picnic tables an didn't see a friendly face, so he took his lunch tray and wandered out to the very edge of the campus green, which was bordered by a low stone wall.

Sitting there, he noticed as he approached, was a solitary figure – a girl in torn, faded, very tight jeans and a Cure tee sheet. She was listening to a Sony Discman.

Marianne! Brandon's face lit up.

Wielding chopsticks, she picked at a plastic tray filled with take-out sushi.

'Marianne!' Brandon called out happily.

'Hi.' She slipped off her headphones.

'What are you doing sitting way out here?'

'This is my reserved table,' Marianne said with a self-deprecating smile.

'Mind if I sit down?'

'Go for it.'

Brandon sat next to her, balancing the tray on his knees. 'Great party the other night,' he said.

She gave him a sidelong glance. 'I thought you had a lousy time.'

'Uh-uh. I meant the part where I met you.'

'Oh . . .' Marianne looked down, as if she were studying something very important on her sushi tray. 'Thanks'.

Brandon took a deep breath, then plunged ahead. 'Listen, would you like to go to Paris for the weekend? I think if we leave Friday night, we can make it back late Monday morning. We'll only have to miss a couple of classes.'

Marianne considered the proposition. 'Seriously?'

'Uhhh, well . . . No. Not seriously.'

But Marianne was considering it *très* seriously. 'We *could* do it, you know. I mean, it *is* possible.'

Brandon's brain blazed: What *wasn't* possible for a rich kid at West Beverly? He grabbed her wrist before she could snag another morsel of fish. 'No, no. I was *kidding*! Really.' He gave her a lopsided grin. 'Why don't we save Paris for another weekend, and go someplace, uh, more local. Like Saturday night, like around eight? . . .'

Marianne shrugged, but to Brandon she looked pleased. 'Sounds great. You know where I live.'

'Excellent.' Brandon wasn't just pleased, he was *jazzed*. He leaned in closer to her and whispered seductively. 'Want to trade for a peanut butter and jelly?'

Marianne laughed gaily, taking a bite out of the sandwich Brandon was holding up.

Unexpectedly, Brandon left the sandwich dangling from her mouth and jumped up, leaving the tray forgotten beside her. 'See you Saturday at eight,' he called out, running excitedly towards the newsroom.

*

Brandon fairly burst through the door of the newsroom,

abuzz with deadline activity, and headed straight for Andrea.

'Hey, know any good places to go for dinner?' he asked without preamble. 'Like for Saturday night?'

For just the tiniest fraction of a second, Andrea thought he meant to ask *her* out for Saturday night, but then she saw the fevered look in his eye.

'Wait a second.' Andrea cleared her throat. 'Where's the article on toxic waste? I'm holding page one for you . . .'

'Don't worry, I'm into it,' Brandon replied cavalierly. 'All I need to do is connect with Mister Ridley to get some Chem facts.'

It wasn't what an editor – *any* editor – liked to hear. 'Come on! We're on deadline here!'

'Hey.' Brandon backed up a step. 'Don't get excited, I *know* about deadlines.'

'Tomorrow,' Andrea said curtly, 'or I write it myself. It's *my* reputation on the line.'

'Okay.' Brandon held up both hands, palms up, in a conciliatory gesture. 'No sweat.' He paused a moment. 'So, uh, why weren't you at Marianne Moore's party the other night?' he asked, trying to restart the conversation on a friendlier keel.

'Brandon, I don't go to parties,' she replied waspishly, as if the answer should have been self-evident to a dodo.

Brandon looked puzzled. 'Why not?'

'Because hanging out with a bunch of people acting stupid, and getting plastered like your good friend Steve, isn't going to get me into the Ivy League.'

'And that's it, that's what it's all about? There isn't anything for you besides school?'

Andrea shrugged. 'Who's got the time for anything else but school? I also do ten hours a week of community service . . . the Ivy Leaguers love that.'

'Uh-huh. Yeah, right.' Brandon gave a to-each-his-own shrug. 'Well, Senorita Zuckerman, hasta luego.'

He turned to go, but Andrea called after him. 'Moonshadows,' she said.

'Huh?' Brandon turned back, a perplexed look furrowing his brow. 'Moon what?'

'A restaurant in Malibu. Near the ocean. Real romantic.'

Brandon brightened. 'Hey, thanks.'

Andrea's voice lowered to a near whisper. 'Someone special?' she asked quietly.

'I don't know,' Brandon replied hesitantly. 'She could be.'

As she watched him leave, Andrea felt a twinge of something she convinced herself was *not* jealousy. She shook off the feeling and resumed her work.

Chapter Nine

Saturday night, and in the Walsh house the bathroom that Brandon and Brenda shared looked like the Nieman-Marcus cosmetics counter after an earthquake.

Make-up, lotions, perfume, astringents, soaps, creams, cotton balls and tissue wads were scattered across every inch of counter space. As her mother walked in, Brenda, in a twinkly black minidress, was peering into a lighted magnifying mirror, applying her make-up.

Seeing how much make-up her teenage daughter was wearing, and how much older and sophisticated the minidress and heels made her seem, both amused and appalled Cindy Walsh.

'This place is a disaster,' she observed.

'It's just the way I keep things organized,' Brenda replied through pursed lips, putting on a coat of dark lipstick.

'You didn't wear this much make-up in Minneapolis,' Cindy frowned.

'Looks hot, doesn't it?'

'You don't *need* a lot of make-up, dear.'

'Mom! This is Beverly Hills. You gotta be a little

glamorous,' she declared, eyeing her mother, who wasn't wearing any make-up, in the mirror. 'You can borrow any of my make-up if you want.'

Cindy ignored the implication. She tried one of the lipsticks out. 'Whose party is it this time?' she asked.

'Don't know,' Brenda said, blotting her lips.

'Kelly driving?'

'Mm-hm.'

'Get the address from her, won't you, dear?'

Brenda shot her mother an exasperated glance. '*Mother*! . . . Parents in Beverly Hills let their kids go where they want, do what they want. They're treated like adults.'

Cindy put the lipstick down. 'Except they're not. *You're* not.'

Through the open window came the heavy beat of loud rock music. A familiar horn beeped.

Brenda resorted to the one argument she knew would work. 'Mom, you know you can trust me. I'll leave you Kelly's number. Okay?'

The horn sounded again. Brenda gave her mother an air kiss, careful not to smear her lipstick. 'Bye,' she said, racing out.

'Home by twelve,' Cindy called out after her. 'I'm serious.'

'Twelve forty-five,' Brenda shouted back from the stairs.

'Twelve-fifteen!'

The front door slammed. Cindy sighed. Picking up Kleenex, she wiped the lipstick from her mouth.

*

As Brenda headed towards the Beemer, she passed her brother, who was heading out to his old car.

'Hey, look at you!' she exclaimed, stopped by the sight of Brandon in his best sportsjacket and slacks. 'Where are *you* going?'

'I got a date,' Brandon replied, trying to sound casual.

'Who with?'

'Marianne Moore.'

Brenda pursed her lips and whistled softly. 'Wow! Careful, kid. I heard she got arrested for going topless on Zuma Beach.'

The horn sounded a third time, impatiently.

'Who told you that?' Brandon asked irritably.

'C'mon, Brenda,' Kelly yelled.

'Just a sec,' Brenda shouted back, adding coquettishly, 'Oh, I hear things.'

'From who?' Brandon nodded in the direction of the red BMW. 'Those stuck-up friends of yours? Careful, Bren, the air's pretty thin up there.'

'You're just jealous because I actually *have* some friends,' she retorted. 'I told you, you're not going to become Mister Instant Popularity out here, Brandon. It takes work.'

The temperature between them was rising rapidly. 'Since when did you become such an expert on "popularity"? You didn't have a single friend in Minneapolis that wasn't *my* friend first!'

'That's a lie, and you know it!' Brenda shot back. 'I've gotta go.'

And without another word, she turned and marched to Kelly's car, while Brandon climbed into his. Both car doors slammed angrily.

*

Chapter Ten

The Blue Iguana was just like any other trendy Hollywood club – decorated in neon pastels and ultra-hip fifties kitsch; owned by a consortium of rock and movie stars, which gave it that certain cachet; and guarded by an enormous, taciturn doorman whose word, when it came to the crucial question of who actually got in, held total sway.

Earrings, purses and hips all swinging, Brenda, Kelly and Donna – dressed to the nines, at the very least – clicked their way from the parked BMW to the Iguana's neon-lit entrance. With Kelly in the lead, they marched past the waiting crowd of hopefuls and approached the doorman together.

'Just a moment, ladies.' He held up one slab-like hand. 'Let's see some I.D.s, please.'

Feigning surprise and some irritation, they began to pull out their licences.

'Give us a break,' Donna muttered.

'Give *me* a break, sweetheart,' the doorman replied.

Brenda was first with her identification; she thrust the

altered licence into the doorman's outstretched hand.

He studied it, looked up at Brenda, back down at the licence, then handed it back to her. 'Okay,' he growled, 'you're in.'

Vindicated, Kelly and Donna smiled. Brenda gave them an excited little la-dee-dah wave and entered the club. 'See you guys inside,' she called out, disappearing into the darkness beyond the door.

Regally, Kelly placed her licence in the doorman's hand. He peered down at it, then abruptly handed it back. 'Sorry, honey.'

'*What*? Do the addition, buster!' She shoved the licence back at him. 'I'm twenty-one.'

'Yeah, uh-huh.' Wetting a sausage-like finger, the doorman rubbed the birthdate away. Beneath the smudge was Kelly's real date-of-birth.

Slowly, the doorman looked up. 'This is what they tell me to do with fake I.D.s,' he growled, tearing the licence into little pieces.

'You slime!'

The doorman gave her an evil smile. 'Come back in about five years, honey.' He dropped the shredded licence into her hand.

'Damn!' Donna swore.

Donna backed away, pulling Kelly along with her. 'Brenda!' she called out. 'Brenda!'

But it was too late. Brenda was already inside.

*

Mulholland Drive, high above the twinkling city lights, was a two-lane blacktop that snaked along the spine of the Beverly and Hollywood Hills. With its many twists and turns and scenic vistas, it was the perfect road for lovers . . . or motorcyclists.

With Marianne driving, and Brandon behind her holding on for dear life, the Harley took the tight curves at frightening speeds.

'Want to drive?' Marianne yelled into the wind.

'I don't know. I mean, it's your dad's bike and everything.'

'C'mon, you'll love it,' she said, pulling over.

They switched places, and Brandon, who'd never before driven anything but a family car or motorbike, puttered off nervously down the winding road.

Marianne reached past him, putting her hand on the throttle. 'Now release the clutch,' she shouted, and as he did, she gunned it. The bike roared into the night and Brandon's heart leapt into his throat.

'You're doing great!' Marianne yelled, whooping wildly into the on-rushing wind. 'Just lean into it a little!'

But as he did, Marianne stuck her tongue into his ear. The bike swerved, but Brandon muscled it back under control.

The wind whipped his face. He could feel the blood pounding in his veins.

*

Inside the crowded, dimly-lit nightclub, the music pounded in Brenda's ears.

She worked her way through the packed dancers to the little bar at the back, where the drinkers were jammed three deep, then manoeuvred her way through the crowd, back to the front door.

A man – male-model handsome and preppily attired – watched with some interest from the bar while Brenda spoke to the doorman inside.

He couldn't hear the conversation, but he could tell the pretty girl in the black minidress was upset, and the doorman wasn't doing anything to help her. With a decisive motion, he downed his drink, put the glass down on the bar and crossed to her.

'What's the problem?' he asked when he reached her. Startled, she jumped, staring at him with huge dark eyes, like a deer caught in approaching headlights.

'Hey, relax.' He flashed his friendliest, most reassuring smile. 'I'm not going to bite or anything. It's just that . . . you look so upset.'

'Well, I *am*,' the pretty girl said with a very appealing mix of tremulousness and forthrightness. 'My friends . . . ditched me.'

'That sucks,' the man said forcefully, and Brenda finally took a good look at him: handsome in a poster-boy sort of way; well turned-out in an expensive, tailored jacket and tie; and she had to admit she found his mix of directness and sympathy, well . . . very appealing. 'Can I buy you a drink?' he added.

'Oh no, I mean, I think I better call my—' Brenda caught herself. She smiled up at him. 'I better call a cab or something.'

'C'mon. One drink.' And persistent, too, she thought. I'm a nice guy. Honest.'

'Welll . . .' He took it for a yes, smoothly taking her by the elbow and guiding her back to the bar.

'What'll it be?' the bartender asked, taking a swipe at the counter in front of them with a towel.

'What'll it be?' the poster-boy repeated, giving her a suave smile.

'Okay. Hmmm.' Brenda was trying to remember the name of a sophisticated drink. 'I'll have . . . uhhh . . . Let me see . . . Hmmm.'

He laughed. 'It's not a trick question.'

Brenda said the first thing that came into her head. 'Banana daiquiri.'

'Interesting choice,' he said, clearing his throat. 'I'll take a Tanqueray and tonic.'

The bartender began to make their drinks. Brenda looked around, then back at the man next to her, and caught him giving her the kind of look that men gave Kelly. Brenda decided she was flattered. She returned his endearingly shy, smitten smile.

He held out his hand. 'I'm Jason, Jason Croft.'

'Brenda,' Brenda said, 'Brenda Walsh.' When she shook his hand, he held it just a fraction of a second longer than necessary.

'So, are you in school?'

Brenda nodded.

'Where do you go?'

'Guess,' Brenda said to give herself time to decide how to answer.

'S.C.?'

Brenda shook her head from side to side.

'UCLA?'

'Right,' Brenda heard herself saying.

Jason's face brightened. 'That's where I went to law school.'

'Really?' Brenda was anxious to change the subject. 'Are you a lawyer?'

'Mm-hm.' So, he was a lawyer, and the look he was giving her was still *intense*.

'Do you live in a dorm?' he asked, not taking his eyes off her for a second. 'Or in a house?'

'A house,' Brenda said brightly. What an odd question, she thought.

'Which one?'

This confused her thoroughly. 'Which . . . *house?*'

'Yeah,' Jason said. 'I know all the sororities there.'

'Ohhh . . . Uh, it's a new one. We all just transferred from Minnesota.'

'State?'

'Yes,' Brenda replied directly, hoping she was making *some* sense.

Jason looked thoroughly perplexed. 'So . . . the whole house just transferred from Minnesota State to UCLA?'

'Something like that.'

'How weird.'

Just then, the bartender brought their drinks over. Brenda took a quick sip, saving herself from further reply.

*

To one side loomed the imposing Moore Mansion, dark and still; to the other, the glittering L.A. nightscape. Viewed from the perspective of a steam-wreathed hot-tub, with a pretty girl at his side and a champagne flute at hand, life in Beverly Hills didn't seem so bad after all, Brandon thought.

Marianne was singing along to some French pop star playing over the outdoor speakers. Brandon was completely mesmerized.

Abruptly, she reached over and pulled a hair on his chest. 'You've got a hair,' she laughed in that lusty, uninhibited way of hers.

Brandon looked down. 'Two actually. I've been cultivating them for about a year now.'

Marianne leaned over and kissed him. 'I think you're really nice,' she said.

Desire and discomfort tumbled around togthter inside Brandon's head. 'I think you're really nice too,' he replied stiffly.

Marianne kissed him again, this time hard on the mouth. When she pulled away, there was a wicked gleam in her eye. 'I know what, let's take off all our clothes,' she said, reaching around to remove her bikini top.

'Wait.' Without thinking, Brandon grabbed her hands.

Marianne looked genuinely puzzled. 'What's wrong?'

'I don't know.' Brandon was confused by how uncomfortable he felt. With difficulty, he articulated the voice in his head. 'I feel ... like, uh, our roles got reversed somewhere. I mean, aren't you supposed to hold out on me a little bit?'

'Why wait?' Marianne's glance encompassed the empty grounds, the quiet house. 'Nobody's stopping us.'

'But what's the rush? I'm not going anywhere.'

'Sorry,' Marianne shrugged, as if she hadn't meant to offend him.

'Don't be,' Brandon replied, squeezing her hands and looking into her eyes. 'It's just that ... I'm having a great time just being here with you. Is that weird?'

'No,' Marianne replied slowly. 'It's just ... most guys expect more from me.'

' "Most guys" want a lot of things they can't get.'

Marianne's rueful smile was tinged with sadness. 'Not in *this* neighbourhood.'

Brandon smiled back, finding himself wanting to comfort her. 'Didn't your mother teach you about playing hard to get?'

This time her laugh was hard-edged and cynical. '*My* mother? She probably thinks *I'm* a prude.'

Brandon didn't understand. 'Wait a second. You mean she—'

'Brandon, my dad manages rock bands,' she said levelly. 'He met my mom on the road. She was this major groupie. They did things in the Seventies and Eighties that would blow you away. I mean, they think my life's a total bore.'

'Wow.' Brandon tried to wrap his boggled mind

around *that* lifestyle. 'You should try spending some time with *my* parents. It would probably feel like a maximum security prison to you.'

'Might be a nice break from this place,' Marianne said wistfully. 'I just feel . . . so trapped sometimes.

'The minute I go out and have fun, everybody at school calls me this major party girl. And then, when I want to be left alone, or just be quiet, they call me stuck-up.' She shrugged. 'Sometimes I think I just can't win.'

She seemed so vulnerable. Brandon reached for her. 'C'mere.'

She pushed him away. 'No.'

The look on Brandon's face made her giggle. 'Isn't that what I'm supposed to be doing?' she asked, all wide-eyed innocence.

Brandon pulled her towards him again. This time, she moved willingly into his arms.

Steam billowed around them. The city lights twinkled below.

'This is really beautiful,' Brandon whispered. 'Years from now, I'm going to look back on this night and kick myself for being such an idiot.'

Marianne kissed him. Gently. 'No you won't,' she said softly. 'I won't let you.'

*

Two banana daiquiris later, Jason opened the door of his one-bedroom condo not far from Westwood and flipped on the light.

Brenda stepped in. 'Wow. You live here all by yourself?' she gushed.

'All by myself,' Jason said.

Brenda was impressed. 'How cool.'

Jason grinned crookedly. 'Listen, I'd offer you something to drink, but I'm all out of bananas.'

Brenda was still pondering the avid look on his face when, abruptly, he took her by the shoulders, pulled her close and kissed her.

Brenda pushed him away. 'Our housemother is very strict,' she said in a breathless rush. 'I've got to be home by midnight.'

He took her in his arms again. 'Don't worry, Cinderella. We're only a few blocks from campus.'

He kissed her again, and this time . . .

Brenda kissed him back, relaxing in his arms, until . . .

She felt his hands fumbling for the zipper at the back of her dress. She pushed him back. Hard.

'What are you doing?'

He grinned. 'Taking off our clothes,' he said matter-of-factly, loosening his tie and beginning to unbutton his shirt.

Brenda was very frightened. 'No, Jason. I can't.'

Jason looked at her as if rejection was an alien concept. 'Why not?'

'I just can't,' Brenda said with all the firmness she could muster.

To her relief, Jason began to button his shirt back up. 'Hey, relax. I can respect that. I don't want to go any faster than you do.'

'Relief' was too simple a word for what Brenda felt. '*Really*?'

'Really.'

He looked at her so sincerely and so intensely that Brenda found herself apologizing.

Jason stopped her. 'There's nothing to be sorry about. I think you're very sweet.'

Slowly, deliberately, careful not to frighten her, Jason bent over her and kissed her lightly on the lips. 'And *very* attractive, too.'

Again, his lips brushed hers. 'And if you want to go, I'll drive you home right now.'

'Thanks,' Brenda whispered gratefully.

*

Jason's Saab cruised slowly up sorority row, while Brenda pretended to look for her house.

'That's it,' she pointed. 'That's the one.'

Jason squinted into the dark. 'I think that's a church,' he said.

'No, not that,' Brenda said in a rush. 'I meant the one next to it.'

Jason pulled over to the kerb, reached into his wallet and took out a business card.

'Here's my number,' he said, holding out the card.

When she reached for it, he pulled it back. 'Listen, are you sure you're not lying about not having a phone?'

Brenda gave him a wide-eyed, who-me look. 'Honest,' she said.

'Okay.' He handed her the card. 'I'm sorry you couldn't spend the night.'

Desire and discomfort tumbled through her mind too. A worried frown crossed her face. 'Me too,' she said, kissing Jason on the cheek. 'I'll talk to you soon.'

And as quickly as possible she was out of the car. 'Hey,' Jason called out to her, 'I think you should work on getting a phone. Communication's important.'

'I'll work on it,' Brenda replied, turning away and walking up to the sorority house. Halfway up the sidewalk, she turned and waved goodbye.

When she was right at the door, he finally pulled away. Brenda waited a moment, until she was certain he was gone, then she turned around and marched back to the street.

*

The taxi glided to a stop in front of the darkened Walsh house. Brenda jumped out, paid the driver and ran to the front door.

Just as she was about to put the key in the lock, someone grabbed her from behind. Turning in terror, she began to scream, but . . .

It was Brandon.

'What are you doing home so late?' he asked mildly.

She hit him on the arm. Hard. 'You scared the hell out of me!'

Brandon rubbed his upper arm. He looked around. 'Lose your ride?'

'None of your business. What are *you* doing home so late?'

'None of your business,' Brandon repeated mockingly.

They looked at each other a moment, then simultaneously, both said, 'Don't tell Mom.'

*

Sitting up in bed in her nightshirt, Brenda could see the first rose light of dawn. For the hundredth time she glanced down at the phone in front of her. Biting her lip, she reached down, picked up the receiver and dialled.

'Kelly?' she whispered.

In her darkened bedroom, Kelly sat up groggily and snapped on a light. '*Brenda?*' She squinted at her alarm clock. 'It's six in the morning!'

'I know. I haven't been able to sleep all night. I had to call you.'

Kelly yawned. 'That jerk at the door wouldn't let us in to find you.'

'I know. You won't believe what happened . . . I met a guy after you left.'

All of a sudden, Kelly was *very* awake. 'No way! Who is he?'

'His name's Jason and he's twenty-five. A lawyer. And he's *so* cute!' Her voice lowered. 'We had a *really* great night together.'

'You slept with him?'

'No . . . But he wanted me to.'

Suddenly there was a knock at Kelly's bedroom door. Without waiting for an invitation, Kelly's mother came in. She was an X-ray Beverly Hills sophisticate, who more than once had been mistaken for Kelly's older sister.

'Just a sec,' Kelly said into the phone. 'It's Jackie.'

'Who *is* that?' her mother hissed.

'Just a friend,' Kelly replied sullenly.

'What kind of friend calls in the middle of the night?' Jackie Taylor snapped. 'She woke Bob up.'

'Good,' Kelly snapped back. 'It's about time *somebody* did. All he does around here is sleep anyway.'

'How dare you talk to me about my life that way! I thought we had an agreement. I let you do your thing, you let me do mine. Right, Kelly?'

Kelly's voice was tinged with sadness. 'Right, Mom.'

That was all her mother wanted to hear. 'Good. Now tell whoever it is you'll call them back in the morning. I don't like this phone-ringing business at six in the morning.'

'Okay, Mom.'

Kelly waited until she was gone and the door was closed to whisper into the phone. 'Still there?'

'Yeah,' Brenda whispered back on the other end of the line. 'What happened?'

Kelly sighed. 'My mom . . . it's nothing.' She brightened at the prospect of more dish. 'So, Brenda, does he know you're in high school?'

'That's just it . . . I told him I go to UCLA.'

'Brenda! I don't believe you! . . . Do you think he has a friend?'

'I don't know, I guess I can ask . . . Kelly, what am I going to do?'

It was one question to which Kelly knew the answer. 'Have a good time,' she said. 'That's what I always do.'

CHAPTER ELEVEN

Another morning at West Beverly High and, in the parking lot, the treacherous beat-the-bell-for-a-spot races were underway ... BMWs, Mercedes, Jags and vintage T-Birds all manoeuvring for the few remaining parking places.

Kelly nosed the red BMW into the last empty space on the entire lot, right next to Steve Sanders, who was just getting out of his smashed Corvette.

Kelly stopped to gawk at the dents. 'Steve, your car ... It's all smashed up. Ooh, *disgusting!*'

Steve slammed his car door. 'Gee, Kel. Thanks for pointing that out to me,' he replied sarcastically. 'I *never* would've noticed.'

Kelly blithely ignored his bitter tone. 'Did you do it? Or was it that dork driving you home after the party?'

Steve's eyes gleamed with the possibility of vengeance. '*What* dork?'

'Oh, I don't know. Just some geek.'

'What's his name? What did he look like?'

Kelly looked surprised. 'Don't *you* remember? He was driving your car.'

Steve shook his head. 'No,' he admitted. 'I was pretty messed up.'

'Well, whoever he was, he looked pretty young, a freshman maybe. He probably didn't even have a licence.'

'I'm gonna find him.' said Steve through gritted teeth, 'And then I'm gonna kill him!'

*

Steve stalked the halls, fixing each passing freshman with an evil glare. Passing a row of lockers, he didn't even notice the one tiny figure with his back to him, huddled shivering against his open locker door.

As Steve swept past oblivious, David gave a little silent prayer of thanks, then rushed to class as the final bell rang.

*

Brenda and Kelly were the last to arrive in Chemistry as the bell rang. The room was already filled with students, seated with papers in front of them.

Mister Ridley immediately strode over to their table and put a sheet of paper in front of each of them. 'Welcome, ladies,' he said with unmistakeable malicious glee. 'You're just in time for a pop quiz.'

'Oh, no!' Brenda moaned under her breath.

Ridley returned to the front of the room, where a CD player sat in the centre of his desk. He stabbed the Play button and classical music filled the air. 'Papers will be due at the end of the movement,' he said, closing his eyes and making vague conducting gestures with his hands.

Brenda and Kelly looked down at the questions; their perplexed looks said it all. 'I hope you know this stuff,' Kelly whispered.

'I haven't studied all week,' Brenda replied.

'Uh-oh,' Kelly gulped.

Students wrote furiously as the music built to a crescendo. Kelly and Brenda worked slowly, their faces studies in confusion and misery.

The music slowed, becoming more languid. The end was near. 'Don't be fooled by appearances,' said Mister Ridley. 'Chemistry, like music, is always tricky, and never what it seems.'

*

In Spanish II, Brandon was seated between Andrea and Steve as the class went through a series of drills, reciting past imperative verb participles in Spanish.

'*I must have been fishing*,' the class chorused.

'*They must have been fishing*,' their teacher said, and the class repeated, '*They must have been fishing*.'

'*We all must* . . .'

The knock on the door interrupted her in mid-sentence. A delivery man, obviously Latino, entered carrying a large bouquet of flowers.

'Si?'

'I, uh, got some flowers for . . .' He fumbled in his pocket for a card.

Miss Montes De La Roca cut him off. 'En Espanol, por favor.'

The delivery man shrugged and smiled, realizing he'd stumbled into a Spanish class. Then, in flawless Spanish, he said, '*I have a floral delivery for Brandon Walsh*.'

Brandon couldn't believe he was hearing his name.

'*You may sign for the flowers, Brandon*,' Miss Montes De La Roca told him in Spanish.

Brandon didn't understand. 'Huh? No comprende.'

The delivery man sauntered over and held out his

clipboard. 'She wants you to sign for the flowers, man,' he said.

Embarrassed, Brandon scrawled his signature. 'Muchos gracias,' the delivery man said, waving to the class as he strolled out, 'Adios, amigos.'

Brandon was left holding a huge bouquet of roses. The teacher walked briskly to him and pulled one of the roses out. She held it up to the class.

'*What is this, class?*'

'Rosa,' they said in unison.

She gave the rose back to Brandon and went to the blackboard, resuming the verb conjugation.

Brandon was just looking at the card, when Steve snatched it from his hand. He gave it a quick scan, then, almost reverentially handed it back. In a stage whisper, he intoned, 'Man! You must've been *awesome*!'

*

Brandon was at his desk in the newspaper office, trying to find a drawer big enough to hold the bouquet, when Andrea came in.

She cast a jaundiced glance at the profusion of roses in Brandon's hand. 'I see your date went well,' she said drily.

'Yeah, I guess,' Brandon said sheepishly. He picked out a single blood-red bloom and handed it to her. 'Thanks for the suggestion,' he said.

Andrea held the rose up in the light, looking appraisingly at its delicate petals. 'Funny,' she mused, 'I just don't see you two together.'

'Why not?'

'I don't know,' Andrea shrugged. 'You seem smart and down-to-earth. And she's kind of . . . stupid and rich.'

'That's not true at all,' Brandon shot back with a flash of anger. 'Nobody really knows her.'

Andrea couldn't help but like that he came to Marianne's defence. 'Well, what's she like?' she asked mildly.

'I don't know.' Brandon's brow furrowed. 'It's sort of like she's got all this money, all this freedom . . . and I think it gets in her way.

'She's got this image that's not exactly her—' That was something that Andrea could sympathize with. 'And then guys go out with her expecting something. And then she doesn't want to spoil the image, you know? So she feels kinda . . . obligated . . . to be this person she's not.'

He looked up at her – intense, serious, sincere. 'Does that make any sense?'

Andrea nodded, impressed despite herself. But because she, too, was trapped in an image that wasn't exactly her, she aded wryly, 'Maybe you should write for our advice column.'

She handed the rose back to him. 'Thanks anyway, but I'm allergic.'

*

Lunch time was always dish hour at West Beverly, but today's was especially spicy.

Kelly and Donna were huddled around an outdoor pay phone. Brenda was between them, dialling.

'Okay,' she said, 'this is his voice.'

She held the phone up, and Kelly and Donna bent their ears close to listen to the voice on the answering machine.

'Hi, it's Jason. I'm not in right now to take your call, but if you'll leave your name, number and the time of your call, I'll get back to you just as soon as I can. Thanks for calling, and remember, wait for the beep.'

In her sexiest voice, Donna whispered, 'Hi, Jason.'

Brenda quickly slammed the phone down. 'Did it beep?' she asked accusingly.

'Nope,' Donna giggled.

'It better not've.'

Donna held up two fingers. 'Swear to God!'

Brenda took a deep breath. 'I'm gonna call him at work.'

'Go for it, honey!' Donna said.

Brenda took out the business card and dialled, while Donna and Kelly watched anxiously.

'Jason Croft, please,' Brenda said in her most grown-up voice. 'Brenda Walsh ... Yes, I can hold.'

*

In another part of the school grounds, an angry Steve Sanders was dishing something else ... xeroxed flyers with a stick-figure drawing of a kid standing next to a Corvette. The word *DORK* was written diagonally across his face.

Steve shoved the flyer into the hand of every passerby, willing or not. 'Fifty bucks if you can help me nail this dude ... I'm lookin' for this freshman dork who was drivin' my car after Marianne Moore's party ...'

David and Scott watched him pass by. David was still wearing shades and a porkpie hat.

'You can take the disguise off,' Scott suggested. 'If he hasn't I.D.'d you by now, he's never going to.'

'Think so?'

'Definitely,' Scott said. 'And I want my Lakers hat back, dude. You said you were going to bring it today.'

'Sorry, man. I forgot.'

Scott was dubious. 'Bet you lost it,' he said accusingly.

'No. I didn't. I, uh, I think I remember where I left it now.'

'Where?'

David looked sick. 'In Sander's 'vette.'

Scott was horrified. '*David*! My name's sewn into it.'

Suddenly, a huge fist thrust a flyer between their heads. 'Fifty bucks, guys. And you can help me kick his ass.'

Scott took the flyer in a trembling hand, as Steve rumbled away.

'I'm history,' Scott moaned.

*

Lap after lap, Brandon jogged around the school track. A kid he only knew by sight as someone on the varsity football team caught up to him, matched strides and ran alongside.

'Hey, you the guy Marianne Moore sent flowers to?'

'Yeah,' Brandon replied between breaths.

'Yo! Robinson!' the kid called out to someone behind them. 'This is the guy!'

Robinson was the quarterback. He pulled up next to them. His arms and legs were like muscled pistons. His head was bald.

'Marianne sent you flowers?' He glared down at Brandon.

'I don't know if you'd actually call them *flowers*,' Brandon said nervously.

'What did you *do* with her, man?' Robinson growled. 'I happen to cultivate a very deep interest in the female species, so I just want to know: *what* you did, *how* you did it, *where* you did it and how you got her to do it.'

Brandon and the two varsity football players jogged on, their footfalls perfectly matched as they went around the track.

'Look, Robinson,' Brandon said at last. 'All I can say is, I did something with Marianne last Saturday night that most guys probably couldn't handle.'

'Yeah,' Robinson said hoarsely, 'what's that supposed to mean?'

With the clarity that comes from a runner's high, Brandon replied, 'Use your imagination.'

And then he picked up the pace; the football players fell behind, lost in fevered imaginings.

'No way, man!' he heard Robinson call out behind him. A small smile played on his face.

When he got back to the locker room, Brandon spied Robinson at the centre of a small group of varsity jocks. They all looked impressed as Brandon passed.

'Yo,' one of them yelled out. 'Heard how you scored with Marianne Moore. Congratulations, man!'

They all laughed, and Brandon laughed with them. Finally, he was in with the in-crowd.

CHAPTER TWELVE

KWBH was blasting *Wild Thing* when Brandon and Brenda pulled into the school parking lot the next morning.

Brenda gave her brother a sidelong glance. 'I heard about you and Marianne,' she said insinuatingly.

'From who?' Brandon turned the car into the lot.

'The whole school is talking about it,' Brenda shrugged. 'I'm surprised at you.'

Brandon brought the car to an angry screeching stop. 'You don't know what you're talking about. Get outta my car!'

'It's not *your* car,' Brenda replied calmly. 'It's half *my* car.'

'Well . . . then get outta my half!'

The song on the radio stopped suddenly, midway through. '*We interrupt this song for a* Wild Thing *Report*,' the D. J. growled. '*Eric Patton and Lucy Belson . . . John Addison and Sarah Takamoto . . . And, the newest, wildest things at West Beverly High . . . Drum roll please . . .*

'*Brandon Walsh and Marianne Moore!*'

Brandon groaned. He turned to his sister. With a smug expression, she hopped out of the car and slammed the door in his face.

*

Brandon walked the halls, feeling the eyes of the other kids on his back, hearing the whispers as he passed. A group of freshman girls dissolved in giggles as he walked by. Some dude he didn't even know slapped him heartily on the back.

'Hey, bud, I'm in your American History class, and I want to hear all about it.'

Brandon was more than depressed. He felt betrayed . . . by himself.

As he rounded a corner, he saw at the end of a long hallway . . .

Marianne.

Brandon was riveted to the spot. His first impulse was to turn and run. But he knew he couldn't.

She walked towards him, briskly, her face showing not a trace of emotion.

'Hi, Marianne.' The grin on his face felt lame and forced.

She didn't reply. He thought she was going to walk right by him, ignoring him, cutting him to the quick. But it wasn't that easy.

As hard as she could, Marianne punched him in the stomach.

'*Liar!*'

Brandon doubled over, clutching his gut, gasping for breath.

'How could you go around spreading that rumour? You—'

'I had nothing to do with it!' With some difficulty, Brandon straightened. 'I swear!'

'You're just like every other creep! You used me to get a name for yourself.'

Brandon held up his hand. 'I swear, I didn't say anything.'

'Then who did, huh?' She looked up at him, inches from his face. 'I really thought I could trust you, Brandon . . . Do you have any idea what it's like not be able to trust *anyone*? Even your own parents – who're always too busy, or out of the damn country, to care about your life?'

She started to walk away, then turned on him. 'I didn't want anything more from you than to have a friend at this school. I mean, a *real* friend. Silly me, I even thought you could use one of those too.'

'I did. I mean, I do.'

Marianne shook her head sadly. 'The funny thing is, they wouldn't have believed the truth anyway. I just feel so stupid right now because I thought you were for real.'

'I . . .' Brandon stopped. There was nothing he could say.

Marianne gave him a brave, bitter, little smile. 'See you at the next party.' She shrugged. 'Who knows? It'll probably be at my house.'

*

There was a knock at the door of the Vice Principal's office.

'Come in,' said Jack Clayton.

Miss Montes De La Roca entered hesitantly. 'You wanted to see me, Jack?'

The Vice Principal stood nervously. 'Please.' He indicated the chair. 'Sit down.'

'Is there a problem?' she asked as she sat.

'Yes . . . sort of.' The Vice Principal seemed unusually nervous. 'The "non comprende" factor has gone sky high this year,' he said, adding, after she continued to stare at him, 'None of your students can understand you.'

She replied angrily in Spanish.

'Whoa.' Jack stopped her with a raised hand. 'See, that's just what I'm talking about.'

Miss Montes De La Roca stood again. 'I'm sorry, Jack, but the only way to learn Spanish is to *live* Spanish, *breathe* Spanish, *feel* Spanish.' She reached over, took his hand in her own and put it on her chest. '*Touch* Spanish. Comprende?'

'Si. I mean, yes,' he replied, flushed and flustered.

She released his hand and smiled enigmatically.

The Vice Principal cleared his throat. 'If their scores don't improve by the end of the month, we'll talk again.'

She turned towards the door without a word.

'Friday night?' the Vice Principal quickly added.

She turned, a slow smile spreading on her face.

'I mean, uh, dinner.'

'I'll let you know,' she replied imperiously.

As Miss Montes De La Roca left his office, Jack Clayton's secretary gave her a gimlet-eyed look that mixed suspicion and disapproval. Two waiting students exchanged a look.

*

As Brandon took his Spanish II seat, Steve gave him a high five. 'Hey, man, you're a legend.'

It wasn't what Brandon wanted to hear, but it was nothing compared to what he heard next. As Miss Montes De La Roca stepped into the room and went to the head of the class, Andrea Zuckerman appeared at Brandon's side. Her face was a mask, frozen and cold fury.

'For once, just *once*, I thought . . . here's a nice guy, a guy with class, intelligence, sensitivity.' Her words were daggers, aimed straight at his heart. 'But now . . . I think you're just a gutless wimp who probably can't even write a good lead.'

'C'mon, lay off,' Brandon sighed, totally dispirited.

But she was having none of it. 'There are better ways to get popular than advertising your sexual conquests! . . . Boy, was I wrong about you.'

She was about to sit, but Miss Montes De La Roca didn't let the outburst pass. 'Senorita Zuckerman. En Espanol, por favor.'

Andrea took a deep breath. Pointing at Brandon, she said in Spanish: '*Marianne Moore sent him roses, and he stepped on her heart.*'

*

In the parking lot, Scott was peering into the back of Steve Sanders' Corvette, while David was watching to make sure the coast was clear.

'I see it,' Scott exclaimed excitedly. 'It's wedged under the seat.'

From under his jacket, David produced a coat hanger. 'Don't worry,' he said, 'I watched my dad do this once.'

He jammed the coat hanger between the closed window and the door frame. Twisting it around, he reached the lock, caught it and yanked it up. The door opened with a satisfying click and . . .

An ear-shattering alarm screeched! David pushed Scott into the car. 'Go!' he yelled. 'Go!'

*

'Beep! . . . Beep! . . . Beep!'

Miss Montes De La Roca stopped in mid-sentence. Heads craned all around the room.

'Oh *no*!' It was an angry cry of pain and it came from Steve Sanders, who was holding a car-alarm beeper in his hand. A stricken look twisted his face, and without another word, he jumped up and dashed out of the classroom.

*

Inside the 'vette, Scott was tugging frantically at his beloved Lakers cap, trying to dislodge it from underneath the seat.

Standing tensely by the open door, David looked over his shoulder and thought his eyes would explode:

Steve Sanders, crazed and screaming, was charging across the parking lot!

'Scott,' David said with as much forced calm as he could summon, 'I think you'd better hurry.'

'It's stuck,' Scott grunted.

David gulped. 'It's Steve.'

Scott sat bolt upright. His head slammed against the roof. '*WHAT??!!*'

It was too late. Steve was bearing down on them, a maniacal killer's gleam in his eye. 'Don't move!' he bellowed. 'You're dead!'

For a moment time was frozen. 'OhmyGod,' Scott whispered. David wondered what the coroner would tell his parents.

Then, from some primitive part of David's brain, came the urgent message: *Run!*

David bolted, inadvertently slamming the door on Scott, who was still struggling to get out.

Twenty yards away and about half a second later,

David stopped and looked back, just as Steve reached the Corvette and pulled Scott, who was clutching the Lakers cap as if it were a lifeline, out by the scruff of the neck.

'You're the guy who drove me home!' Steve roared, slamming Scott against the side of the car.

Scott was hysterical. 'No! It wasn't me! I swear it wasn't!'

David's mind didn't believe it – he was safe – but his legs were carrying him back. He stopped at the far end of the car.

'You got the wrong guy, jerk!' David heard himself saying. 'It was *me*! I'm the one who drove you home that night!'

Confusion washed the killer grimace off Steve's face. 'Huh?' He looked down at Scott, who was starting to cry, then back at David, who, come to think of it, *did* look kind of familiar.

'Remember?' David prompted, his voice rising to the upper registers. 'We kinda hung out together. I told you how I was this big fan of your mom's? And then I drove you home 'cause you were too wasted to do it yourself.'

Steve stared blankly at David, then the memories came rushing back. 'Oh, yeah ... *You're* gonna pay, buddy!'

He let Scott drop, moving single-mindedly towards David, who began backing away. They began to circle the car.

'You were gonna drive *drunk*! I did you a favour, man!'

'*So*,' Steve shot back belligerently, 'what happened?'

David was still backing away; Steve was still stalking him. 'After I dropped you off, I forgot to put the car in gear. I'm not used to driving stick.'

Steve stopped. He groaned. 'Oh *God!*'

David stopped too. 'Okay, I admit it, it was my fault,' he said in a rush. 'I may have to work at McDonald's the rest of my life, but, somehow, I'll pay for it.'

'Moron.' Steve took a deep, shuddering breath and exhaled slowly. 'I've got insurance.'

David came closer; he actually began to relax. 'Hey, I know this guy in the Valley who works on 'vettes real cheap. If you get a good quote from the insurance company, you could actually make some money on the deal.'

'Really?' Steve looked interested. David fell into step beside him and they began to walk together towards school.

'Yeah, man,' David said blithely. 'You can buy yourself some new speakers.'

Steve stopped abruptly. 'What's wrong with my speakers?' he asked suspiciously.

'I don't know,' David shrugged. 'I guess I was jammin' the sounds pretty loud. Maybe I blew a tweeter.'

'Oh, man!' Steve's lip curled, as if he found himself face-to-face with a particularly repellent piece of garbage. 'What did I do to deserve meeting a total dork like you?' And then he turned away and marched back towards the school.

But David wasn't so easily insulted. 'Hey, see you at the next party!' he called out cheerfully. A moment later, what he'd actually just done sank into his fevered freshman brain and he collapsed against the car.

Scott, who'd witnessed the entire scene from the vantage point of the ground where Steve had tossed him, finally pulled himself up and perfunctorily brushed off his precious cap. 'That is the studliest thing I have ever seen,' he declared.

'*We are cool*,' David agreed. And the two intrepid freshmen exchanged an exuberant high five.

*

Tuesday night at the Walsh house, and the smell of pot roast wafted through the air.

In her room upstairs Brenda stood in front of the mirror, absentmindedly combing her silky hair and practising being an adult.

'Hi,' she said brightly to her mirror image, 'I'm Brenda.'

No, that wasn't it.

'Hello,' she tried again, more soberly, 'I'm Brenda Walsh.'

Not that either.

She took a deep breath and tried it once more. 'Hi, I'm Brenda . . . er, Walsh.'

She gave her reflection a cross frown. 'I *hate* my name,' she declared, catching a glimpse of her brother leaning against the doorframe and looking at her as if she'd lost her mind.

'Bren, what're you doing?'

Brenda transferred the cross look from the mirror to her brother. 'Don't you *ever* knock?'

Ignoring the remark, Brandon walked in and plopped down on his sister's bed. 'Can we talk for a second?' he asked.

Brenda looked dubious. 'About what?'

'I don't know.' Brandon shrugged, 'Just talk. Ever since we moved here, we hardly talk to each other . . .' He paused, then blurted out, 'Don't you ever miss Minneapolis?'

Brenda resumed combing her hair. 'Not particularly,' she said.

'All our friends.' Brandon said softly, his voice tinged with sadness, 'The places we used to hang out. Parties at our house, staying up late and talking . . .'

'*Brandon*, I really don't want to take a trip down memory lane right now,' Brenda snapped, brushing her hair with irritated vigour. 'I've got a date.'

Her brother looked surprised. 'With *who*?'

For just a second the brush hung in the air as she said, 'He's . . . older.' A strange smile flickered across her face.

'In college?'

Brenda finally turned away from her reflection. 'Something like that. But if you tell Mom—' She shook the brush emphatically in his direction, 'I'll kill you.'

'Hey, I won't say a word,' Brandon hurriedly reassured her. 'I swear.'

Brenda seemed mollified. 'Okay then.'

'Listen, I want to ask you about something,' Brandon said, his eyes lowering and his voice dropping to a confidential whisper. 'That rumour that's been going around about me and Marianne. I don't know . . . I kinda feel responsible, like I started it somehow, because I never really denied it.'

He looked up, hoping to hear at least a few sisterly words of consolation, if not a brilliant solution to his dilemma, but was amazed to see . . .

Brenda wasn't even listening. She was appraising her reflection in the mirror.

'Hello . . . Brandon to Brenda: anybody home? . . .'

Brenda glanced down, as if coming out of a trance, and saw the clock. 'OhmyGod! I'm late! I'm late!'

She grabbed Brandon by the arm, dragged him off the bed and pushed him out of the room. 'Go on, go! Hurry! I've gotta change.'

'Yeah, sure,' Brandon said glumly, turning to stare at her closed door.

*

Brandon was just sitting down to dinner with his parents when Brenda came tripping down the stairs. Brandon articulated what his flabbergasted parents were thinking: his sister looked . . .

'Incredible! Wow, Bren!'

With all the make-up, her usually straight hair combed out to incredible proportions and her short, tight, off-the-shoulder minidress hugging every curve of her figure, she looked like a Rodeo Drive starlet.

'Brenda,' Cindy Walsh fluttered, 'I'm only making pot roast.'

'Oh, didn't I tell you,' Brenda trilled, with the utterly innocent expression that her brother instantly recognized as meaning she was trying to put one over on their parents. 'I'm going out with some friends tonight.'

'On *Tuesday night*?' Jim Walsh frowned mightily. 'Don't you have homework?'

'We're studying afterwards,' Brenda said casually.

Something on, or rather *near*, the floor had caught Cindy Walsh's rapt attention. 'Aren't those *my* shoes?' she asked wonderingly, gazing down at her most expensive, dressiest and highest heels.

Brenda just gave her mother her winningest smile, as if to say, and don't they look just great on *me*, huh Mom?

The frown on her father's face had gained additional valleys. As always, he cut to what was for him the bottom line. 'Where's all this "dinner money" coming from, anyway?'

'It's just McDonald's,' Brenda said lightly, giving her

father the smile treatment, too.

'In *that* outfit?' her mother asked dubiously.

Brenda, her brother noted with a somewhat professional interest, now resorted to the aggrieved and unjustly accused routine. '*Mom*! This *is* Beverly Hills! God, can't I have some friends without getting the third degree.'

That got 'em, Brandon noticed, as his parents exchanged an exasperated look that signalled imminent surrender.

'Back by ten,' Jim Walsh said gruffly.

Brenda knew when to declare victory and skip out. 'Ten-thirty,' she called out gaily over her shoulder.

'Ten-fifteen,' her father shot back as the front door slammed. He turned to his wife and with a puzzled look. 'I haven't even *seen* a McDonald's around here,' he said.

Brandon took a sudden interest in his pot roast, staring down at the plate so his parents wouldn't see the broad, amused grin plastered on his face.

CHAPTER THIRTEEN

L.A. is the City of Trends, and nowhere is this more apparent than in its restaurants.

With the regularity of a bird migration, and with just as mysterious a telepathy, word spreads among the city's Beautiful People that the place to *be*, and to *be seen*, this week is the new Japanese place on trendy Melrose, or the new French Provincial bistro on La Cienega's Restaurant Row, or, perhaps, the latest pastel California eatery specializing in nouvelle cuisine that just opened on Main in Santa Monica.

For the next two weeks, or the next two months if the restaurant's lucky, the limousines and the paparazzi and the movie stars and studio heads *must* all show up, and all *must* have a good table (that is, one that's better than wherever they spot their supposed peers). And for those few heady weeks, the maitre d' is turning them away by the droves and booking weeks in advance. And then, just as suddenly as it came, the tide of Beautiful People recedes, and it's on to somewhere else.

But tonight, a half hour after declining the pot roast, Brenda found herself with Jason and his two best friends, Alison and Ron, being ushered to a very good table in *the* noisy, jammed, ultra-hip restaurant of the absolute moment.

She recognized half the clientele from movies and TV, and the other half, strangely enough, looked as if they recognized *her*. Or, anyhow, thought they should.

Alison was in her mid-twenties, thin, hyper, extremely put-together. And Ron, in his late-twenties, was obviously her boyfriend, and a colleague of Jason's at the firm.

They were both dressed casually chic — the kind of casually chic that's very studied and very fashion-conscious — and sitting with them, Brenda was excruciatingly conscious of how over-dressed she was. It didn't make struggling with the pasta any easier, particularly given how adept they all were with their spoons.

'So, Brenda,' Ron said, 'what's your major?'

Alison gave Ron a proprietary smile. 'Don't you get so sick of everyone asking you that?' she asked in a silky tone.

Sitting across from her, Jason chimed in. 'What is it, anyway?'

Brenda found herself sucking up a dangling noodle strand before she could reply. 'Astronomy,' she replied as casually as she could, looking at each face around the table in turn.

Their pleasantly polite expressions gave way to looks of surprise.

Alison looked at Jason through half-lidded eyes. 'Wow, you didn't tell us she was a brain, Jason,' she gushed in a breathy whisper.

'I flunked astronomy,' Ron said glumly.

Jason was impressed. 'I didn't know you were majoring in astronomy,' he beamed, looking directly into her eyes.

Brenda shrugged, as if she'd been cataloguing the heavens all her life.

Alison made a kind of little girlish face — *very* high-school, Brenda thought, not to mention a cheap way to get the men's attention again. 'It's *so* much math,' Alison said, casting another coquettish glance in Jason's direction.

Brenda was amazed to feel Jason's hand squeezing hers under the table. 'Hey you guys,' Jason said casually to the table at large, 'you like this Pinot Grigio?'

'Good,' Ron intoned.

'*Very* dry,' Alison purred.

Jason ignored her. 'You like it, Brenda?'

'Mmm-hmm,' Brenda nodded, taking a sip.

'Let's order another bottle,' Jason said expansively, waving to a passing waiter.

Ron leaned in towards Brenda. 'I heard they discovered *another* universe,' he said as if imparting a confidence. 'After this one. Like a billion light years away, or something like that.'

Brenda looked back at him, a frozen smile on her face.

Alison shot her boyfriend an irritated, tipsy glance. 'Who *cares*, Ron?' she snapped.

'Well, I'm sure *Brenda* does,' Ron huffed. 'It *is* her major. I mean—' He turned back to Brenda. 'What *is* a black hole, *really*?'

Jason had finished with the waiter and twisted back in his seat. 'Tell us, Bren,' he encouraged casually.

Brenda was definitely on the spot and found herself wishing she hadn't had her full share of the wine. 'Well, if you *really* want to know.' She stared back at the inquisitive three faces bobbing up and down. 'Umm, I guess the easiest way to explain it, without a working knowledge of, ummmm, fourth dimensional geometry, is . . . that . . . it's like a hole, in space.'

Ron screwed his face up, trying to grasp it. 'Just a hole, huh?' he said wonderingly.

'In space, dummy,' Alison snapped.

'That's black,' Brenda added helpfully.

Ron shook his head slowly, in rapt amazement at the wonders of science. 'I still don't get it,' he said.

Alison rolled her eyes heavenward, as if seeking divine intervention, or at least Brenda's sisterly sympathy, with this oafish cross she had to bear. Relieved, Brenda gave her her most sympathetic smile.

Alison smiled back. 'So, Brenda,' she said. 'Jason tells us your entire sorority house transferred from Minnesota.'

'Well, not exactly.' Brenda lowered her eyes modestly. 'Just five of us really.'

Alison's eyes flashed at Jason. 'I *told* you, Jason. It was *not* the entire house.'

'Well, that's what she said,' Jason protested, but Brenda squeezed his hand back under the table. Jason stammered that he must've misheard and soon the conversation moved on to more innocuous things.

*

It was getting steamy on sorority row, so steamy in fact that the windows of Jason's parked Saab were entirely fogged over.

Inside, Brenda and Jason were making out, wrapped in each other's arms.

Reluctantly, Brenda pushed him away. She took a deep, shuddering breath. 'Curfew,' she sighed. 'I just gotta go.'

Jason's flushed face was covered with lipstick marks. Eyes burning at her and breath ragged, he nodded at her, as if he had to gather himself before he could even speak. 'Let's go out Friday night,' he said at last, between shallow gasps. 'Just the two of us. I've got a real special place in mind.'

Brenda's eyes were big and liquid. 'Okay,' she said softly, kissing his cheek. 'Goodnight.'

'And make plans to spend the night,' Jason called after her. 'Tell your housemother you're . . . I don't know . . . visiting your parents for the weekend.'

Brenda flinched at the word 'parents,' but tried not to let him see. 'I'll try,' she said.

'Try hard,' Jason said heatedly.

Brenda waved, forcing a wan little smile. She watched as he pulled away. When he'd rounded the corner, she took a deep breath and walked to her own car.

Chapter Fourteen

Midweek morning at West Beverly High. Hump Day, they called it, because once you survived Wednesday you could coast into the weekend.

Hump Day was the kind of day where everybody expected just to get by. Last weekend's shocks and scandals had been put to rest, Monday's school traumas had resolved themselves into the steady grind of midweek, and Friday was far enough away that it would take another twenty-four hours before the adrenaline would begin to pump.

Just another ordinary Wednesday morning with students pulling into the parking lot, lugging armloads of book into school, waiting impatiently for friends to arrive. Of course, everybody was tuned to . . .

'It's the High Sound of West Beverly High! C'mn at ya!. . .' The D.J.'s gravelly voice lowered to a confidential whisper. *'An' we got a very special guest in our KWBH studio today!'*

In a tiny booth crammed with audio boards, records, tapes and CDs, Brandon sat jammed next to the D.J., a funky-looking kid with spiky hair who went by the name of Flash.

'*Yes, yes, it's none other than Brandon Walsh, the new kid on our block, an' this week's ... Wild Thing! He's just moved from Minnie-apple-iz to the Hills o' Beverly, and already he's gettin' with the programme, y'understand? ... Say hello to our listeners, Brandon.*'

Brandon leaned into his microphone. '*Hi,*' he said softly.

Outside, unseen but felt, they were *all* listening:

Steve tuning in, in his battered Corvette ...

Kelly bringing up the volume in her red BMW ...

Marianne screeching to a halt in her Mercedes 560 SL and shaking her head in amazement ...

'*Tell us, Brand-man,*' the Flash growled in his most insinuating voice, '*just what does it take to be a Wiiiiild Thing?*'

'*Um, actually that's just what I wanted to talk about—*'

'*Whoa, whoa, whoa! Before you do, Br an-dude, before you say another word, jus' remember: we are regulated by both the FCC and Mrs. Sibitsky, our esteemed club sponsor!*'

Brandon took a breath, struggling to master his conflicting emotions. '*Okay ... Look, as long as my date with Marianne has become ... public knowledge, I ... I ... I mean, you guys out there should know what* really *happened between us that night.*'

Steve whooped, slapping the 'vette's dashboard with the palm of his hand. 'Awright, my man!'

Kelly, sailing into a parking space, just smiled.

Two aisles away, Marianne was gripping the wheel so tightly her knuckles had turned white.

'*Oh, yeah! We're all ears, Bran-baby! ...*'

'*Okay.*' Brandon took another deep breath. '*Well, basically . . . this is it:*

'*Nothing. I mean, nothing happened.*'

The Flash looked more than surprised. Even the spikes in his hair seemed to be wilting. '*Uh, Brandon . . . The key phrase here is "Wild Thing."*'

In her car, Marianne was hanging on every word.

'*Yeah, I know that,*' Brandon's voice was saying through her speakers. '*But listen: All we did that night was talk, just talk.*'

'*Like, you mean . . . talk?*'

'*Yeah . . . and you know, it may sound a lot less exciting than doing the Wild Thing, but, you know, it actually meant a lot more.*'

Marianne's hands unclenched. She smiled.

And in the studio, Brandon leaned even closer to the microphone and in a low whisper said, '*So, anyway . . . I hope you're listening, Marianne, 'cause, well . . . I just want to tell you, I'm sorry. And the thing that bums me the most is that you don't think you can trust me anymore . . .*'

This wasn't the dirt the Flash had bargained for. He jerked the microphone away from under Brandon's nose. '*And that appears to be all the time we have this morning for mushy declarations of love.*'

*

Wednesday was lab day in Chemistry class. Classical music wafted through the air. Steamy wisps wafted from beakers on the benches. Mister Ridley alternated between passing out papers and conducting an imaginary orchestra with a ruler. Kelly and Brenda watched a coloured beaker of fluid cooking over a bunsen burner's blue flame.

'With very few exceptions,' Mister Ridley exclaimed in his fluty voice, '*most* of you did very well on the quiz.'

Brenda and Kelly weren't listening. They weren't even paying much attention to their bubbling beaker. It was what the pop psychologists called Life Lessons that concerned them today.

'Jason wants to go out again Friday night,' Brenda was saying. 'He wants me to spend the night.'

'You've got to tell him, Brenda,' Kelly said emphatically.

Brenda found herself doing something she hadn't done since eighth grade. She was distractedly chewing her nail. 'What if he freaks?' she asked in an intent whisper.

'Science is about observations, class,' Mister Ridley was intoning, as if from far away. 'So, pay attention to the music.

'If you're doing your experiment correctly, your hydrogen should bond with the sulphuric acid *exactly* when the first movement ends.'

'If he really loves you, it shouldn't matter,' Kelly advised. 'Do you think *you* love him?'

'I don't know,' Brenda replied morosely.

'Enough to sleep with him?' Kelly asked quickly, cutting through to *her* bottom line.

'I don't know . . . I think so.'

'Then you've got to tell him,' Kelly declared in a then-that's-that tone.

A shadow fell across their beaker. Unsmiling Mister Ridley handed them their quiz papers.

Brenda looked down at her grade and was stunned. It was as if he'd flung the beaker in her face.

'Very poor showing, girls,' Mister Ridley was saying, as Brenda's brain bubbled like the chemicals in the beaker on her lab table. 'It's also very disconcerting to observe that you both share *all* the *wrong* answers in common.'

God, how could I have let this happen!

'If I ever see that kind of thing again, it's an automatic 'F' for the year.'

Kelly's face was an impassive stare, but Brenda was stricken.

'I've taken the liberty of making an appointment for you with Mister Clayton, Brenda,' the Chemistry teacher droned on.

It took a moment for the words to sink in. Brenda's voice quavered as she plaintively asked, 'Why?'

'I've seen the transcripts from your former high school,' Mister Ridley replied impassively. 'I expect much more from you in this class than a D minus.'

Silence descended on the Chem lab, then . . .

'*Thwack*!'

Brenda, her nerves already excruciatingly on edge, jumped in her seat as Ridley's ruler came down next to her on the desk. 'Now,' he called out, turning away, 'the movement's over. The experiment has ended.'

*

Brandon, books under one arm, his other hand jammed in his jeans pocket, was loping through the halls when he spied Marianne at her locker.

'Hi,' Brandon said, approaching her tentatively.

'Hi,' Marianne replied, adding in a studiously neutral tone, 'I heard what you said this morning.'

Brendon felt his face flush. 'I guess I made a fool of myself in front of the entire school.'

'I hope so,' Marianne said.

Brandon thought he had that coming. He sagged

against her locker. 'I . . . I want you to know I never meant to hurt you, Marianne . . .'

She shrugged, blasé, as if to say, *nothing* can hurt *me*. 'You just saw an opening and you took it.' Again that world-weary shrug that hurt Brandon more than a slap in the face. 'I never meant to let you get close to me.'

Brandon stiffened. 'No, don't say that,' he implored. 'Please, give me a second chance. How about Friday night?'

'No,' Marianne said firmly, but without any rancour. 'I think I'm going to do something kind of weird this weekend.'

'What?' he asked suspiciously. What could be 'weird' for a girl like Marianne, who'd seriously considered just popping over to Paris for the weekend?

Her eyes twinkled; her features softened, as if just the thought made her feel more carefree. 'I'm staying home . . . A rare event.'

Brandon smiled. 'It's a good idea,' he said, nodding approvingly. Sometimes the world could be such a surprising place, he thought. 'What about the week after?'

And as if to prove just how surprising it could be, Marianne suddenly stood on tiptoe and kissed him. 'I'll call you,' she said lightly, then skipped away.

Brandon was left standing alone in the hallway, grinning crookedly and shaking his head. 'Great,' he muttered wryly to himself. '*She'll* call *me*.'

*

Knees together, hands clasped together in her lap, Brenda sat on the very edge of the chair, facing Vice Principal Jack Clayton across his desk.

His head was lowered as he studied the transcript –

her transcript – in front of him. The only sounds in the quiet room were the low hum of the air conditioning and the dry hiss as he turned the pages. Brenda felt as if she could barely breathe.

So *this* was what it felt like to be the kid called into the Principal's office. She had never given the possibility the slightest thought; it was something that could never happen to that model student, that paragon, Brenda Walsh.

But *that* Brenda Walsh had lived in Minnesota, spent her summers on Big Boy Lake, studied every school night, never snuck out or lied to her parents about where she was going, barely gave boys a second thought. *This* was the Beverly Hills Brenda Walsh . . .

At last, Jack Clayton looked up, staring squarely at her. 'I don't get it, Brenda. You've never even gotten a C before . . . What's up?'

'Nothing,' Brenda said. The word came out a sullen whisper.

'Brenda,' he said earnestly, 'when I see a good student come to my school and slip like this, I feel responsible. What can I do to help you?'

'Nothing.' Again that whisper. She hated the way she sounded to herself.

Jack Clayton tapped his index finger against his pursed lips, then, in a no-nonsense tone he said: 'Brenda, from the way things are going, you'll be lucky to pass Chemistry this semester. That's not going to look very good on your record.'

'I know,' Brenda said quietly, looking down. 'I'll work harder.'

'That's a girl,' he replied, his voice filled with confidence and support. 'I *know* you will.'

And then, to Brenda's dismay, he scribbled something down on a piece of paper and handed it to her.

'What's this?' she asked.

'Have one of your parents sign it and bring it back to me,' Vice Principal Clayton said briskly.

She couldn't keep the alarmed quaver out of her voice. 'W-why?'

'Because *something* is going on with you, Brenda. And I want to make damn certain that you're talking to somebody about it.'

Brenda had to fight hard not to cry.

*

As always, Wednesday seemed endless, but finally the last seconds ticked away and the bell rang.

It was like a dam breaking; a wave of kids broke out of the front door and poured down the front steps. Brandon spotted Andrea near the head of the crowd.

'Hey, Andrea!' he called out.

She turned, gave a noncommittal little wave, then kept going. Brandon ran to catch up to her.

'Hey, didn't you listen to KWBH this morning?' he asked without preamble.

'I *never* listen to KWBH,' she shot back without at all lessening her stride.

Brandon was walking at top speed to stay even with her. 'So you didn't hear what I said? About Marianne?'

'No.' Her tone was clipped, unyielding. 'And frankly, Brandon, I'm not interested.'

Brandon grabbed her arm, pulling her to an abrupt halt. The river of homeward-bound students divided around them. 'I want to explain something,' Brandon said.

But Andrea slipped free of his grasp. 'Sorry, I've got to get home.'

'Wait,' Brandon called after her. 'Can I give you a ride?'

'No, thanks,' she shouted back.

Frustrated, Brandon watched her go. It wasn't fair, he thought, he deserved at least to be heard... And he *would* be!

Checking over his shoulder to see what direction she was taking, Brandon raced towards the parking lot.

He reached his battered old Honda, lost a few precious seconds fumbling with his books and his keys, got the door open at last, threw the books in, hopped behind the wheel, clicked on the ignition and... gunned it!

He went racing down the streets, glancing from side-to-side, searching for Andrea.

'Damn,' he muttered. Where could she be? He didn't question *why* it was so important to find her and reverse her harsh opinion, he just knew that it was.

*

Nobody walks in L.A., went the song lyrics popular a few years ago, *Only nobodies walk in L.A.*

And around West Beverly High, that was especially true, just as it was true that only nobodies – like the Hispanic maids clustered around the RTD stop a few blocks from school – took the bus in L.A.

But that was exactly where Andrea could be found, seated in the uniformed maids' midst, waiting for the bus that went into Hollywood. And stranger still, all the maids there seemed to know her and had greeted her arrival with familiarity and warmth.

Every few seconds, Andrea checked her watch and looked behind her; it was the furtive look of someone who doesn't want to be seen.

Finally, the bus arrived, pulling up to the stop with a hydraulic sigh. One after another, the maids stepped aboard. Finally, with one last furtive glance around, Andrea, too, got on. Just then . . .

The Honda came screeching around the corner, just in time for Brandon to catch a glimpse of Andrea dropping coins into the farebox at the front of the bus.

As the bus pulled away, the confusion on Brandon's face gave way to a look of determination. He followed it.

'Where the hell is she going?' Brandon said aloud as the bus headed East.

Inside, in the back of the bus, a group of the maids was giving Andrea her daily advanced Spanish language lesson.

Through Beverly Hills, past West Hollywood, then into Hollywood proper, and still the bus headed East, until finally . . .

Andrea got off in a neighbourhood of small, but neatly kept bungalows, deep in *old* Hollywood, a part of the city that hadn't known glamour or wealth since the late 1930s. She said 'adios' to two of the maids, who had gotten off with her, then trudged up the small cobblestone walk leading to her home, just as a car pulled up in the driveway next to her and beeped. Andrea turned, and was absolutely stunned to see Brandon waving at her.

'*You*! You followed me! I don't believe it!'

Brandon turned off the engine and got out of the car. 'Hey, it was the only way to talk to you.' He looked around, giving the little neighbourhood the once-over, just your typical tourist. 'But . . . how did you end up going to West Beverly?' *I* mean, you don't live anywhere near Beverly Hills.'

For once, Andrea didn't instantly know what to say.

'My life is private,' she snapped, rage boiling up in her face. 'How dare you come anywhere near my house!'

Brandon was shocked, not just merely taken aback, by her outburst. 'Hey, I wanted to talk,' he protested.

But Andrea was livid. 'And I suppose you'll go blabbing to everyone about where I live, just like you did about you and Marianne Moore . . .

'*Brandon*,' she said his name sharply, as if it were painful to speak it, 'this isn't a *game* to me. I'm not rich like you . . . If anybody finds out where I live, they'll kick me out of West Beverly High so fast it'll make my head spin.'

'But why,' Brandon asked, choosing his words carefully, 'do you go *there*, if you live . . . *here*?'

With difficulty, Andrea brought her seething emotions under control. 'Because,' she began, in the familiar clipped tones of the school paper's feared editor, 'it's the best school in the city. That's why.

'And why should I be deprived of a good education just because I'm "geographically undesirable"?'

'You shouldn't,' Brandon said with evident feeling. 'You're right.

'But listen to me: the reason I followed you is to tell you that I think you've got me all wrong. That whole thing with Marianne . . . It wasn't me. It's important that you know that. That's not who I am. I mean, I'm not perfect. But I'm not a complete jerk, either.'

Andrea began to calm down. Brandon was so obviously sincere about what he was saying and, she realized, there could be only one reason why he'd made the effort to convince her that he was a true-blue, stand-up guy: *Brandon cared about her opinion of him.* But why? Did it mean he found her attractive? It couldn't be! She shook the thought out of her head.

Andrea gave him a sidelong appraising glance.

'Brandon, I lie about my home address. Okay? My grandmother lives in a cheap, rent-controlled apartment in Beverly Hills. That's where all the mail gets sent.

'If you tell *anybody* about this, it's going to mess me up bad.'

Solemnly, he extended his hand. 'I won't,' Brandon said, looking her directly in the eye. 'I swear.'

For a moment Andrea just stared back. Then she took his outstretched hand, shook it and gave him a shy smile that dissolved in surprise when Brandon, who was feeling the relief of a man reprieved from some particularly lonely dungeon, clasped her in a sudden hug.

'Thanks,' he whispered in her ear.

'C'mon,' she said, nodding in the direction of the house. 'It's nice to finally bring a friend home from school.'

Chapter Fifteen

Friday night in Malibu, the fabled seaside community where the movie stars lived. It was the California Riviera . . .

A moonlit night and a white sandy beach. The susurrant hiss of gentling rolling waves.

A chic ocean-front restaurant, all redwood and glass. Anchors and ship's wheels and knotted fishing nets decorating the walls. A flickering fireplace and a combo playing soft South American-accented jazz.

A candlelit table for two tucked in a corner. Gleaming silver and bone white china, the delicate slivery remains of a pink salmon fillet. Two lovers sipping chilled Chardonnay, their faces flushed with the wine and romance.

'God, Jason.' Brenda murmured, 'This is a beautiful place.'

'For all this money, it better be.' Jason leaned back, stretching in his chair, the very picture of the well-fed diner, but his eyes never left her face. 'But it's worth it, to be here with you.'

Brenda looked down modestly, feeling the flush rising in her cheeks. 'Thanks.'

'I think you're *really* nice, Brenda.' He leaned forward, elbows on the table, lightly brushing her cheek with the back of his hand. 'Can I tell you something? . . .'

Brenda looked up, her eyes catching the candlelight. 'Sure,' she said.

'The last woman I went on three dates with I lived with for eleven months.'

'What happened?'

'I . . . don't know.' Jason's eyes got a faraway look. He was gazing into the past. 'When it got close to our year anniversary, well, we had this weird fight over a new couch for the living room.' He chuckled mirthlessly. 'I guess I had to go with my own taste because I thought the couch might be around longer than she would.' He shook his head at the memory and his eyes refocused, returning to the present, returning to Brenda. 'I guess that sounds pretty shallow, doesn't it . . .' He took another sip of the Chardonnay. 'I don't mean to get heavy on you,' he said with a warm smile.

Now was the moment, Brenda thought. *Now*, or she would never be able to tell him. She swallowed, suddenly feeling very sober, maybe *too* sober. 'That's okay,' she said softly, 'because, Jason . . .' She gazed directly into his eyes. 'Do you think I could tell you *anything*?'

'Of course,' Jason shrugged, as if it was self-evident. 'You know,' he added expansively, 'the older I get, the more I realize *openness* is the most important part of any relationship.'

'You'd still feel that way, no matter what?' she asked with a kind of desperate earnestness. 'This could be a shock.'

'Trust me,' Jason said reassuringly, covering her hand with his own. His light laugh seemed carefree. 'Hey, I'm shockproof.'

Nothing. The words wouldn't come. Brenda sat across from him, mute, lost in the blue of his eyes.

'Brenda, what *is* it?'

As he watched in growing puzzlement, she opened her purse and took out a pen. She quickly wrote something on a napkin and, as she handed it to him, said, 'First of all, I want you to have my phone number.'

Jason's face lit up like a little boy getting candy. 'You got a phone!' he enthused. 'Boy, that's great.'

'No.' The pleased smile flickered. 'I've always had a phone.' Then it vanished from his face.

'You see . . .' She took a deep breath. Now there was no going back. 'I don't live in that sorority house.'

'No?' It was a mild no; a neutral, questioning no; the practised no of an attorney.

'I don't go to college.'

'You work?' Jason asked mildly.

'No, Jason.' And now there was no avoiding it any longer. 'I'm a junior at West Beverly High.'

Jason just blinked at her, a politely inquisitive look on his face, as if she'd just said something in a foreign language he didn't understand. ' "Junior?" What kind of junior?'

She told him with blunt directness. 'A *sixteen-year-old* junior.'

So much for shockproof, Brenda thought. He was holding on to the edge of the table with such force that it appeared as if he thought their little corner of the restaurant was about to sail out to sea.

Brenda plunged ahead. 'My best friend Kelly told me that, since we were getting serious, I *had* to tell you the truth. And – and that if you really love me, it wouldn't matter.'

It seemed so straightforward, so logical, that, for a moment, as she heard herself speaking those words, Brenda was convinced that everything would be alright.

Then, somehow, Jason untwisted his horrified expression just long enough to spit out a reply. 'Oh, is that what *Kelly* said?' His voice dripped with sarcastic venom.

Brenda flinched from the bitter outburst. 'I thought you were shockproof,' she said, just as a hapless waiter approached their table.

'More wine, perhaps?' he asked, bending slightly forward and rubbing his hands together.

Jason shot him a withering look. 'Maybe you should check her I.D.,' he snapped, glaring from the waiter to Brenda. 'I suppose that's fake, too.'

Crab-like, the waiter scuttled away as fast as he could. Diners at nearby tables had paused, forkfuls of food in mid-air, to stare at them.

'How could you do this to me?' Jason hissed. 'What is this, some kind of high-school prank?'

Brenda could feel her eyes filling with tears. 'I'm sorry, Jason. I, I thought . . .'

But Jason was on his feet, nearly upending his chair. 'You thought *wrong*! I should sue your parents!'

He waved urgently for the waiter. 'Check! Excuse me, *check*!'

*

Down the Pacific Coast Highway, with the twinkling lights of the city marking the curve of Santa Monica Bay, and the planes far overhead, circling to land at L.A.X., like trails of golden fireflies . . .

Then along the twisting curves of Sunset Boulevard as it wound through the postcard-perfect communities of Pacific Palisades, Bel Aire, Westwood and, finally, Beverly Hills . . .

The long, romantic ride back should have been the perfect end to a perfect evening, but instead it was the longest, coldest drive Brenda had ever endured. Jason remained totally silent, his face an impassive mask.

'Left here,' Brenda said at last.

Jason made the turn.

'Third house on the right.'

He pulled up at the kerb. Finally, he turned and stared at her. 'Tell me, Brenda.' he said, his face contorted in a sneer and his voice dripping acid, 'Was it fun playing grown-up?'

This time, Brenda didn't have to pretend or strain to find that controlled, that 'adult' tone. 'My feelings for you didn't change just because I'm a few years younger than you thought I was.'

Jason's reply couldn't have been more insulting, or patronizing. 'What the hell do *you* know about feelings?'

'A *lot*,' Brenda declared, surprised to find within herself a voice of such authority. 'I would *never* tell anyone I liked them and then treat them the way you're treating me.'

'Wait until somebody you thought you cared about lies to you,' Jason shot back.

'Don't you think it was hard on me too, Jason? . . . Lying to my family about where I was going at night? . . . Flunking out in school? . . . All for *what*?'

Tears began to course from the corners of her eyes; still, she continued in a clear, strong voice. 'God, I can't believe it! I was actually going to sleep with you tonight, Jason! *You* were going to be the first . . .'

She threw open the car door. 'Oh . . . never mind.'

Her words were electric, sparking a fire in Jason's head. He grabbed at her arm. 'Wait! Maybe . . .'

But she pulled away and jumped out of the car. Quickly, Jason was out of the driver's side and coming around towards her. 'Brenda!'

'No!' she sobbed. Now there was no stopping the flood of tears. 'Get off me! I'm *glad* this happened!'

That stopped him, cooling his ardour as quickly as it had become enflamed. 'At least,' he said tentatively, 'let me walk you to your door.'

'Go away, Jason!' Now her voice was rising almost to a shout. 'I never want to see you again.'

And she turned and ran towards the house. Suddenly, the front door opened and Brenda's mother was standing there, framed by the light.

She shot him a sharp, unmistakeable look, and Jason shrugged, on his face the saddened look of missed opportunity. He turned away, walked slowly to his car, got in and – with one last look at the girl in her mother's arms, the girl he now realized could have been *The Girl* – he drove off into the night.

'Oh, Mom,' Brenda sobbed into her mother's shoulder, 'I'm so sorry.'

'Shhh,' Cindy whispered to her daughter, 'it's alright, honey.'

'I never meant to lie to you,' Brenda got out between sobs, in a voice that was filled with remorse.

'Who is he, Brenda?' her mother asked gently.

Brenda straightened, took a deep breath and wiped at her tear-stained cheek with the back of her hand. 'Oh, just some guy. Kelly and I went to this club and . . .' Her voice quavered again.

But it was enough for Cindy. She knew what her daughter had been going through. 'It's okay.' she said softly, 'It's my fault, too.

'I . . . I knew things weren't right. It's just that I wanted you to be happy, to fit in . . . But not like this.'

Brenda couldn't stifle another sob. 'I know,' she said, the very picture of misery, just as her father came outside.

'What's wrong?' he wanted to know.

'Nothing,' Brenda said in a tiny, sniffling voice, laughing despite her tears at how ridiculous she must sound.

As always, she turned to her mother for support. 'Can we talk about this later? . . . I've got a lot of Chemistry to catch up on.'

'Sure, dear,' Cindy said.

As Brenda slipped between them and went into the safety of the house, Jim turned to his wife, a puzzled frown on his face. 'What happened?' he asked her.

Cindy put her arm around her husband's waist. 'Mother-daughter stuff, Jim,' she said. 'I've got things under control.'

That was something Jim Walsh knew better than to question. He threw an arm around Cindy's shoulder, and together they walked back in.

*

Brandon was in his room, stretched out on his bed and reading, when his sister walked in.

'Hi,' she said.

Brandon arched an eyebrow and grinned. 'Don't you ever knock?' he asked wryly.

Brenda put her index finger to her lips, then made a check mark in the air. 'Score one for you,' she said, smiling ruefully.

Brandon put the book aside and sat up. 'Are you going to tell me what's going on?'

'Ohhhh . . . It's kind of a long story.'

Brandon crossed his arms in front of his chest. 'I'm not going anywhere.'

Brenda sighed, sitting down at the foot of the bed. 'Brandon, do you mind if I save it for when you're older?'

'What do you mean?' He frowned, as if doing a complex calculation in his head. 'I *am* older. By thirty seconds.'

For once, Brenda didn't object. 'I know,' was all she said. 'It's just . . . when you get to our age, girls are more mature.'

'Oh, give me a break!' he began, then remembered Marianne . . . and Andrea, and he thought better of it. 'Okay, if that's the way you want it.'

'Thanks.' She sounded genuinely relieved. 'And someday I'm going to tell you *almost* everything.'

'Forget it,' Brandon shot back quickly, feigning total uninterest. 'I've already lost interest in *your* dull life.'

'I miss Minneapolis,' Brenda suddenly blurted out.

Brandon gave her a sceptical look. 'No you don't,' he said firmly.

Brenda shrugged. 'Nothing was this complicated,' she said wistfully.

All of a sudden, Brandon was *very* curious. 'Brenda, did you . . . ?' It was a question he didn't need to finish.

'*No*,' she replied so emphatically that he knew it was true. 'Did you?'

Brandon smiled. 'No,' he said.

She smiled back at him, feeling somehow vindicated. 'I didn't think so,' she said, standing.

For a moment she just looked down at him – her brother, her best friend. 'Brandon,' she asked, 'are we going to make it here?'

He gave the question serious thought; in fact, it had

been something he'd been wondering himself. 'The houses are bigger,' he said. 'The weather is warmer. And the tan lines . . . they're *outstanding*.'

He grinned. 'But that doesn't mean they've cracked the secret of life – know what I mean?'

Brenda smiled, feeling at peace for the first time in weeks. 'I know,' she said quietly.

Now it was time to get back to work, to resume, being . . . *herself*, the same girl who'd watched the Northern Lights in wonderment on their last Minnesota night. She started back for her own own room, but was stopped by her brother's voice.

'Brenda?'

'Yes?' She turned.

'Would you have told me if you did?'

Brenda's smile was as enigmatic as the Mona Lisa's. Wordlessly, she reached over and turned out his bedroom lights.

As she closed the door behind her, she could hear her brother cackling in the dark.